Deborah Ann Reardon is a North Carolina author. She has had many hobbies since the age of 35, when she was introduced to creativity: painting in many media, pottery, beading, weaving, knitting, rug hooking, quilting, miniature bonsai trees, and more. She enjoyed making up stories for her children when they were young. Several years ago, she wanted to tell her story of struggles from her early life. So, she began her first novel, *Through It All*, which is a fictional biography. After completing that book, she found that she very much enjoyed writing stories and is currently working on her fifth novel.

Dedicated to my four children

Deborah Ann Reardon

Through It All

Thorne Davenport Series –
Book One

AUSTIN MACAULEY PUBLISHERS™

LONDON * CAMBRIDGE * NEW YORK * SHARJAH

Copyright © Deborah Ann Reardon 2024

All rights reserved. No part of this publication may be reproduced, distributed, or transmitted in any form or by any means, including photocopying, recording, or other electronic or mechanical methods, without the prior written permission of the publisher, except in the case of brief quotations embodied in critical reviews and certain other non-commercial uses permitted by copyright law. For permission requests, write to the publisher.

Any person who commits any unauthorized act in relation to this publication may be liable to criminal prosecution and civil claims for damages.

This is a work of fiction. Names, characters, businesses, places, events, locales, and incidents are either the products of the author's imagination or used in a fictitious manner. Any resemblance to actual persons, living or dead, or actual events is purely coincidental.

Ordering Information
Quantity sales: Special discounts are available on quantity purchases by corporations, associations, and others. For details, contact the publisher at the address below.

Publisher's Cataloging-in-Publication data
Reardon, Deborah Ann
Through It All

ISBN 9798889109815 (Paperback)
ISBN 9798889109822 (ePub e-book)

Library of Congress Control Number: 2023920530

www.austinmacauley.com/us

First Published 2024
Austin Macauley Publishers LLC
40 Wall Street, 33rd Floor, Suite 3302
New York, NY 10005
USA

mail-usa@austinmacauley.com
+1 (646) 5125767

Prologue "MeMe"

Here I sit, as I have for the past five years, in the corner on top of her chest of drawers. I can see and hear almost everything, but she doesn't talk to me anymore. I'm not sad though, because I know she loves me and would never throw me away.

I sit among many friends. I guess she likes them and puts them up here to keep me company. All these friends have sentimental value to her because they were given to her by special people, her children. I am the most special because she adopted me, and I am the oldest. She has never shared any of her thoughts and feelings with these friends; just me. I guess that is why I really know I'm special.

I remember when I came to live with her. She gave me life. The hugs and kisses were wonderful. Sometimes I would be her student. She would teach me all the things she was studying. I didn't like the history class too much, but I loved it when she taught me creative things. I could tell her soul was into it.

Another of my favorite times was at night. She would cuddle up to me, making sure I was comfortable, and I would lie there all night listening to her soft breathing and dreams. I don't believe she realizes how much I know about her.

The many tears she shed when pouring out her hurtful feelings to me still are evident in my matted fur. There were so many times I wanted to comfort her with hugs and words, and I think she felt this. She shared her life with me, no matter what was happening. I would sit on her bed or sofa waiting for her return. We went on a couple of trips together. She was never embarrassed to have me with her. I was her real partner in life.

What happened, you ask. To tell you the truth, I do not think she even knows. Time has a way of changing things and people. I have been here listening and watching as she has struggled through many difficult situations, heartbreaks, and confusing times. Through it all, she has finally learned the true meaning of peace, the real relationship that makes life worth living. I know she wants to tell you but does not know how.

So, let me tell you her life's story so that you may get to know and understand this very wonderful, and deeply beautiful person.

Harnett County News
March 23, 1994
Car accident results in death of driver

The fatal accident occurred at 8:45 a.m. today at the junction of Highway 210 and 410. It is believed that the Jeep Cherokee ran the stop sign and T-boned the Nissan Sentry. The driver of the Nissan suffered head injuries and is in serious but stable condition at Betsy Johnson Memorial Hospital in Dunn. The driver of the Jeep was pronounced dead at the scene. Identification is being held until notification to next of kin has been made.

Chapter One
2014

Carly Jansen had graduated from UNC-Wilmington with a degree in English and journalism. After graduation, she returned to her hometown of Lillington, North Carolina, where she rented a small duplex apartment to be near her parents. Her first job had been a proofreader for a magazine company based in Dunn.

Three years ago, the owner of the *Harnett County News*, an old friend of the family, had offered her a part-time position at the paper. Although her job would be more clerical doing general office duties than actual reporting, she would at least be in an environment of journalism. Also, it would greatly reduce her travel time since she would be working closer to home.

Carly Jansen's 34th birthday would be coming up in April, but this year there would not be the usual celebration that her parents had always had for her. Helen and Paul Jansen had adopted Carly as an infant. Carly was their only child and birthdays were big celebrations when she was younger. Since her college days, her mom always made a cake and gave her a gift with a small celebration. She would miss that this year, however. Her mom had died of pneumonia eight months previous, and her dad died of a sudden heart attack just before last Christmas.

Carly had never married. She had a pet, a two-year-old Yorkie-mix named Sunshine PoohDinkle, "Dinkle" or "Sunshine" for short. Carly had felt overwhelmed with gratitude when she learned of her inheritance, not enormous in some people's eyes, but enough to change her circumstances and enable her to work toward fulfilling her dream of becoming a fiction novel author.

With the inheritance from her parents, Carly was able to buy a small house on the outskirts of town and continue working part-time at the newspaper to pursue that dream. She found the perfect little cottage-type, one-bedroom home in Flat Branch, about 10 miles south of Lillington, North Carolina.

Chapter Two

Carly Jansen ascended into the sky once again. At least that is how Dinkle saw it. The doorbell interrupted Dinkle's patient but anxious wait for Carly to descend from the clouds and off she ran toward the front door, barking.

"I'm coming!" Carly yelled, making her way down the creaking attic staircase. "Coming!" she called out once more.

Brushing off the attic dust from her blouse, she opened the door. "Well, hey Nellie! This is a pleasant surprise. Come on in." Nellie Garrett had been a family friend for years and worked at the diner in Bunnlevel that Carly frequented often. It was just outside Lillington.

Nellie handed a paper bag to Carly. "Brought you some multigrain blueberry muffins to give you energy for all the work you are doing. Also, I have a few of your things in the trunk of my car. Thought I'd bring them by and see if you needed any help with getting things unpacked."

Carly took the bag of muffins to the kitchen while Nellie returned to her car to get the box.

Carly met her at the door, got the box from Nellie and took it into the hallway, and placed it near the other unpacked boxes. "Have a seat, Nellie. I'll get us something to drink."

Nellie sat down in the chair close to the patio sliding glass doors. "I don't want to hinder your work. Is there anything I can do to help you?"

"Don't be silly. I have forever to get things sorted through. I need to take a break, anyway. Just make yourself comfortable. What would you like? I have tea, cranberry juice, lemonade, and water."

"Lemonade sounds good." Nellie looked out the patio door. "You have a nice backyard. You could have a nice flower garden, maybe even some tomatoes in the spring."

Carly brought the lemonade and gave Nellie her glass. "It's sweetened with Sweet and Low, hope that's OK."

Nellie nodded and took a sip. "Perfect."

Carly sat on the couch and curled her legs to one side. "I was thinking about a garden too. I'm not sure what to plant exactly. Maybe you could give me some pointers."

Nellie looked around the room. "Looks like you just about have everything unpacked. You must have been working around the clock. How do you like this new house of yours?"

"I just love it. It's quite different from my apartment in Lillington. It's bigger, for one thing. It's very quiet too, a perfect place to write my book someday. The yard is really great."

"You're still going to work at the paper office, aren't you?"

"Yes, still part-time for now. I'm hoping to get into writing articles, you know, real journalism."

After a brief silence, Carly said, "You know Nellie, my parents made all this possible, the house and the job."

Nellie said, "I know you miss them. How are you doing with it all?"

"I have sad days, some not so bad, but overall, I believe I'm OK. You know, Nellie, I am very fortunate that such caring people adopted me. I had a very happy childhood, unlike many adopted children. Mom and Dad taught me some important things about life—honesty, caring about other people, not to be judgmental of others, working hard, those kinds of things. I always knew I was loved by both. I try to think more about the happy memories than the fact that they are gone."

"I'm sure they were proud of you, Carly. It's wonderful that they were able to help you." Nellie sipped her lemonade. "Your parents were up in age a bit when they adopted you, weren't they?"

"Yes, and maybe that's what made them so knowledgeable about life."

"I'm still waiting for the knowledge to hit me," Nellie said, trying to lighten the conversation.

"I never thought about their dying, much less about them leaving 4 me any money. I cherish the sentimental things, my mom's old biscuit pan, and my dad's old typewriter—things like that. I wish they knew how thankful and appreciative I am."

Changing the subject, Nellie asked, "Have you heard from Scott?"

"He's called me a couple of times. I've been so busy trying to get everything in place, I haven't had much time to miss him. He'll be coming back tomorrow."

"It's too bad he had to be away when you could have used his help with the move."

"It wasn't that bad. I enjoy getting everything fixed up and putting things in their place."

Nellie slowly got up from the chair to take her glass to the kitchen. "Sometimes I think this arthritis is going to get the best of me. Of course, I could stand to lose a little weight, which might help the pain in my knees."

To be in her middle seventies, Nellie seemed much younger, always on the go, working at the diner all hours, and helping anybody that needed it. Nellie was one of the most unselfish people Carly had ever known.

Dinkle was snuggled beside Carly on the sofa. Carly rubbed her gently. Dinkle stretched, gave Carly a look of approval, and closed her eyes again.

"You're not working at the diner today?" Carly asked when Nellie returned to the living room.

"No. I've worked a number of days and decided I'd take a couple of days off. Of course, the place will probably close down without me," she said with a chuckle. "At the very least, Ed will be glad to see me when I get back."

Ed Madry had owned and operated the *Green Hornet Grill* between Lillington and Bunnlevel since the 1980s; prior to that, he had sold used cars in Dunn. Nellie had been a waitress, cashier, and cook at the diner since it opened.

"You know, since Ed's wife left him a few years back, he's practically made the diner his home."

"Do you think you will ever retire, Nellie?"

"Well, lately I've been thinking about doing some traveling. I'd like to go up to Ohio and see my hometown, maybe down in Florida, to see my boys. I haven't seen them in a few years." Nellie paused in thought. "As far as retiring, not really gave it much thought. The folks that come to the diner are like family. I guess you could say I don't really consider working there a job. It's just my life."

"Would you travel by yourself? Drive your car?" Carly didn't want to sound as if Nellie was incapable of traveling by herself, but times were changing. The world just was not as safe as it used to be.

"Oh yeah, it would be a good change of pace for me. I've been stuck in a rut for too long. Why not just venture out and do something different?"

"I admire you so much, Nellie. I hope when I get to be your age, I am half as spunky and full of life."

"Speaking of spunky, I came to help you out. What would you like me to do? I can help you unpack some boxes."

"I've got plenty of time to do all that. I just enjoy you visiting with me. You know Bunnlevel is not that far away, so I hope you'll come to see me often. When I get the patio fixed up, you can come over and we can sit outside on nice days. I'll have my birdfeeders set out and we can listen to nature's serenade, drink lemonade, and talk about life. Maybe you can help me with some ideas for my book."

"I like that idea; it sounds fun and relaxing. Well, if I can't help you, I can at least stop hindering you. So, I'll be getting on down the road." Nellie rose and Carly followed her to the door.

"You take care, and you know you can call me if you need anything."

Nellie looked toward the sofa, "Bye Dinkle, you take care of your momma." Dinkle, lacking in social etiquette, kept sleeping.

"It sure is a beautiful day," Carly said as she walked with Nellie to her car, an older model Chevrolet Impala. The car just seemed to fit Nellie's personality, sturdy, well-made, lasting forever. "I'm so glad you came, Nellie, and don't wait for an invite, come anytime."

"You'll still come to the diner, won't you?" Nellie said as she opened her creaking car door.

"Of course, I can't miss out on the latest news in town." Carly liked sitting at the *Green Hornet Grill* in Bunnlevel, listening to the latest news in town, and everyone sharing their opinions while they drank coffee, ate ham and eggs and grits, homemade vegetable soup, apple pie, ice-cream, and many more entrées that didn't meet Carly's health-conscious dietary regimen. "In fact, I have to go into the office Friday, I'll see you then."

Nellie backed out of the drive. She thought of Carly as a daughter. At age 34, Carly was so young and full of life, so innocent. Nellie wondered to herself how someone with such little experience in life could write a book.

Chapter Three

Carly went back inside. Dinkle was waiting by the door. "I guess it's time to get back to work, Dinkle." She took the last box up to the attic. When she pushed the box in place near the rafter post, another box slid from behind the post. It was not one of her boxes. Carly reached for it, pulling it toward her. The box was quite dusty, rather old appearing, and sealed with tape that had yellowed and dried with time. Carly pushed it nearer the staircase opening.

As she backed slowly down the stairs, she propped the box on the steps for support. When finally reaching the bottom, she placed the box on the floor and closed the folding staircase. Dinkle immediately transformed into a bloodhound, sniffing every square inch of the box.

Carly went to the kitchen, got a cloth from under the kitchen sink, and returned to wipe the dust from the box. She used the letter opener that she kept on the mail tray beside the front door to slit the tape around the box lid. Her apprehension was mixing with curiosity. She took the box and placed it on the floor beside the sofa. *What in the world could be in the box? How long had it been in the attic? Who put it there?*

Carly slowly lifted the top from the box. Carefully, she randomly picked through its contents—photos, old greeting cards, stapled papers, folded papers, small booklets, several small binder notebooks, keys, a couple of small wooden boxes, trinkets, a tiny ceramic frog, more photos, a small handmade book of poetry, and several journal-type books.

Carly leaned back on the sofa, contemplating what to read first. She got up, went to the kitchen, and put on the kettle to make some hot chamomile tea. While waiting for the water to boil, she freshened Dinkle's water and opened a can of Alpo Filet Mignon Dinner, his favorite. She spooned a small amount in the doggie bowl while Dinkle patiently waited. After making her cup of tea, she grabbed one of the muffins that Nellie had brought and returned to the sofa to begin the exploration of her newfound treasure. Soon Dinkle joined her.

Carly took a few items from the box. She did not know where to begin. Although some items had dates, there was no sequence to the arrangement of the papers. Most of the papers were old and fragile. Carly carefully lifted a pink piece of paper and began to read:

9-28-78 You know, there's nobody to tell my feelings to. I want to cry. I want to leave. I'm scared about my concert and I'm sad and deeply depressed about my marriage life. I'm so unhappy with him and I don't care about him. I don't think you can love anyone who makes your life so miserable. I can't breathe unless he wants to know why and how deep and how many breaths I take. I know it's not normal I wish I could go to the mountains and just sit until I get my thoughts straight. I love my kids.

Forever it seems I've lived in the storm, sometimes in the wind, most times in the rain. The only calm I know is when I'm in the eye of a great storm.

Carly placed the paper on her lap, sat back, and took sips of her tea. She just stared at the paper, then the box. What had she found? She reached into the box for another folded paper, placed her teacup on the table, and continued to read.

7-24-76 My dear friend!

So glad to hear from you and know that things are going along rather smoothly it sounds. Don't get discouraged and keep your chin up. You are still a young woman and have a good head on your shoulders, just don't let anyone make you think any differently, and don't let anyone (men or women) take advantage of you. Stand up for yourself and what you believe is right.

Enough advice for one time, just remember I believe in you, and I know you can do it—Well, I guess that is about all for now. You take care and tell all the kids I said hi. Write again when you can and always look ahead. Love, Ann, John, and kids.

P.S. Sure do miss having you around.

The postmark was Jacksonville, Florida, but no return address. Carly picked out a few more items. Ticket and parking stub to Universal Studios, picture postcards of the Mohave Desert, a handmade heart-shaped card with a stick of Juicy Fruit gum glued inside printed with the words:

To Mother, from Renee—

I choose you for my Valentine

A day planner from 1976 contained names, numbers, and miscellaneous notes. An entry on 7/23/76 read:

Divorce final, food stamps $198, car insurance for 6 mo. bought car.

A plain blank little postcard dated 4/17/82:

Mom, I just wrote to tell you that I love and miss you! Love, your daughter, Boo.

Carly knew the journey through the box of writings would take days or even weeks. She went to the back porch to get an empty box in which to put the items as she finished looking through them. She looked forward to finding out more about the person who left this box of memories. She studied each photograph and gently placed them in the second box. They were mostly children, a boy, several little girls, school photos, and a few very old black-and-white pictures.

She opened a small cardboard box that contained ticket stubs, a wine bottle cork, and a broken bracelet, closed it, and placed it in the second box. Greeting cards were mostly Mother's Day cards, not dated, and signed, "Love, your daughter" or "Love always, your daughter" and a few happy birthday cards, "Love, brother."

Carly placed them in the second box. Finishing her muffin, she took a few sips of her tea. From the treasure box, she unfolded a few pieces of notebook paper stapled together, and read:

June 22, 1979—Friday 8:00 p.m.

I finally got this book out of my studio. So many times, I've wanted to write my feelings. So much is happening and has happened to me, since February especially. I really plan to write my real feelings here. I hope no one reads this. I left Bruce for the last time. The night before, he raped me and treated me awful. All the pressure was getting to me, I felt like my mind was going to crack. My kids are with him now. I have a big hassle with all I've been taught, how I've been treated, and how I'm living now.

The ice-cream man just came I haven't seen an ice-cream man in a long time. When Sara and Renee come tomorrow, I'll get them some ice-cream. I've had a terrible time adjusting to not having my kids. Nobody knows the pain; I mean the deep pain I've felt since I lost my kids. Bruce has never done anything but hurt me and he talked against me to the kids and got their minds messed up and when my parents talked against me that Monday night, April 9, it convinced my kids their daddy was right.

Melanie and Jeremy wanted to go live with Bruce, and I felt I was losing them anyway, and besides, I couldn't afford them. I was nearly at the point of being committed. I did the only thing I could. I love them so deeply. I want to see them, and I don't want to see them. It makes it so bad for them and me. They don't understand, especially my little girls. Maybe I'll have them again soon or maybe I should say someday. Nobody understands, they all judge and worry about me. Talk to you later.

Dinkle sensed Carly's emotions and snuggled closer, licking Carly on the arm. Carly looked back at the date on the paper, *1978, 1979—almost 35 years ago, she thought, before I was born.* Carly refolded the papers and placed them in the second box. There was no organization or order to the writings. She got up and took her cup to the kitchen and rinsed it.

She originally planned to have a nice long soak in the bathtub, but it was late, and she was too tired, maybe tomorrow night. Carly put Dinkle into his small kennel for the night, gave him a small Milk-Bone, and said goodnight.

Chapter Four

Carly did not sleep very well during the night. Each time she awoke, she checked the time on the lighted clock next to her bed—1:30, 3:00, 4:15, and finally, at 4:40 a.m., decided to get up. She put on her lavender summer robe, reached down, and opened the kennel door. Dinkle followed her into the bathroom and watched Carly brush her hair and wash her face.

In the kitchen, she removed the cover on the doggie door so Dinkle could go and come as needed and she poured herself a glass of cranberry juice. In the living room, Carly sat in the old rocker that had been her mother's; it had been reupholstered several times. The sun would be rising soon. She missed her morning paper. Although she already knew what the contents of the newspaper would be, she still enjoyed her morning ritual of looking through it. Her paper delivery would start in the next few days.

The box of writings filled her thoughts. Reading the papers felt like an invasion of someone's personal life. Dinkle came back through his doggie door and lay down beside Carly's soft bedroom slippers, using the toe end as a pillow. Carly was always quiet in the morning, and so was Dinkle. They sat peacefully, waiting for daybreak.

After a few minutes, Carly, still in her pajamas, went over and sat on the sofa and opened the box of writings. She picked out the book of poems. The booklet was thin, printed, and stapled by the writer or a local print shop, the cover was blue with a symmetrical design, 18 pages, one poem per page. *A rather professional-looking job*, she thought and began reading the first page.

Relief Deep Feelings—
Wish they could be known Who would understand? Forever to live in me alone.
What is happiness and freedom. Not life, I think,
Death only is a real relief.
Belief—not from the inner self, But the outer world
Holding the inner prisoner.

Carly read the poem once more and continued to the next page.

<u>Ingredients</u>
Is the sea made of water? Is the beach full of sand?
Is the desert hot and barren? Is the forest full of trees? Then love is made of pain!

Carly's thoughts turned to Scott. Love was made of pain. Like most girls, she had experienced her first crush, puppy loves, and infatuations. Dating in college was fun but not serious because her mind was on her studies. She had dated a few men since leaving college, but nothing serious ever developed. Her relationship with Scott was more serious, but love? She didn't really know. They enjoyed one another's company, and talked easily about different subjects, but love? She turned the page of the poem booklet.

Past, Present, Future—Painful—my memories are. Effortless—my being seems. Hopeless—my future looks.
Try to forget.
Try to not be conscious.
Try to not dream.

Carly put the poem book on the table and went outside on the back porch for a bit. When she lived in her apartment, she would never go outside in her pajamas, but here she had complete privacy as woods surrounded her backyard and no houses were in view. The morning air felt muggy. The summer seemed to come earlier each year. She wondered why the box of writings was in her attic. Would she be able to find the person who left the box in the attic?

After a while, Carly went back inside, reached down, and gave Dinkle a little pat on the head. She wanted to continue reading the poems and other writings in the box, but she needed to go to town and buy a few necessities. When she had lived and worked in Lillington, trips to the store were very convenient. Although Flat Branch was only 10 miles away from town, she knew her shopping habits would have to change.

Carly took her shower and put lavender lotion on her face, arms, and legs. She blew her shoulder-length, blonde hair semi-dry. Casual clothes for today, she decided and slipped on her size 8 blue denim jeans, pale-blue short-sleeved blouse, and leather sandals.

Dinkle knew Carly was getting ready to leave the house and waited in the hall by the front door to get one last pat and rub. "I'm going to the store. You be a good girl and take care of everything for me. I'll be back real soon, Sunshine."

Carly sometimes wondered what Dinkle did all day. Did she sit by the front door and wait, roam the house, or just rest quietly? One thing, for sure, she was no problem and never did anything wrong. Carly locked the front door behind her.

Chapter Five

As she drove, she listened to the radio, mostly world news headlines and the weather. Hurricane season was approaching. The people in town didn't need the newscasters to remind them of last year's hurricane. Hurricane Fran's damage last September was very similar to Hurricane Diana a little over ten years ago.

Carly remembered both storms. It caused so much anxiety and panic, not only in this area but also in all of eastern North Carolina. She passed the *Green Hornet Grill* but decided not to stop since Nellie wouldn't be there. The National Weather Service was predicting more major storms this year. Carly hoped not. Hurricane Hazel in 1954 used to be the topic of conversation when hurricane season approached.

In recent years, there seemed to be more severe storms and flooding was prominent in the eastern and central parts of North Carolina. The weatherman gave his usual forecast, summer-like temperatures but low humidity.

Carly arrived in Lillington, turned off Main onto a side street where she usually parked. She got out and walked back to Main Street to Barton's Drugstore, the oldest and only drugstore in town. In fact, most businesses in Lillington were the oldest and the only. She exchanged *good morning* with several people passing on the street. The bell rang as she entered the drugstore. After picking out her usual items, baby aspirin, multivitamins with calcium, and toiletries, she went to the checkout.

"Well, Carly Jansen! How are you? I hear you've moved away from us." Ms. Maggie was the oldest and only person to work behind the counter at Barton's Drugs.

"Yes, Ms. Maggie. I didn't move far, though, only about ten miles. You know where Flat Branch is?"

"Oh yes, never been there, but some of my customers live out that way." Ms. Maggie's thin wrinkled fingers hit the number keys on the old cash register, the total key, and then tore off the printed receipt. "Haven't seen Scott around in a few days." Carly knew Ms. Maggie could print her own town newspaper with all the latest town gossip.

"He had to go out of town on business, but will be back later today," Carly informed her.

"Well, we're glad to see you still coming to our place to get what you need."

"Of course, I've shopped here all my life, sure wouldn't stop now. Besides, I'll still be working at the newspaper and Flat Branch is just a little crossroads, not a real town."

"Well, you take care, Carly, and come back real soon."

"I sure will, Ms. Maggie. You take care." The bell rang on the door as Carly left the store. On the way back to her car, she passed Doc Skinner, the town vet, and yes, the oldest and only vet in town. "Hey, Dr. Skinner."

"Howdy Carly, good to see you." He was getting out of his old rust oleum-primed 1964 Ford truck.

"I'm going to call your office soon. It's about time for Sunshine's yearly checkup." Carly spoke louder than usual, as Doc was a little hard of hearing.

"How is the little fellow?"

"She's just wonderful. Doc Skinner always referred to Dinkle as a little fellow. I better be getting back home to her. See you soon."

Dr. Skinner gave a friendly wave.

All Carly could think about on her drive back home was reading more of the writings in the box.

Chapter Six

As always, Dinkle happily greeted Carly at the front door. She put her pocketbook on the hall table, gave Dinkle a rub, and with Dinkle close behind, she took the shopping bag into the bathroom to put away the items she had purchased. "Are you hungry, sweetie?"

Carly put fresh water in Dinkle's bowl and mixed a little *Puppy Chow* with her *Alpo*. She decided to make herself a spinach salad with cucumber and fresh mushrooms topped with Italian dressing, no salt, just a bit of garlic powder. She fixed a glass of lemonade and sat at the bar.

She read the headlines of the newspaper she had picked up in town. The same news for the week; the school board was trying to get more money, a few townspeople were cited for jaywalking, disturbing the peace, loitering, driving under the influence, a couple of comic strips, the obituaries, and want ads. Carly folded the newspaper, took her plate to the sink, added more lemonade to her glass, and went into the living room.

She picked up the poem book once again. The little book did not have a date on it.

Confused
May thoughts, many feelings, which do I obey?
Pulled and pushed,
In every thought and way.
Only the future knows.
I am so confused.
I hope one day it will, without a doubt, be straight.

Just a Little
Not love—just a little affection.
Not marriage—just a little time with me.
Not lies—just truth. Not pity, real concern.
Not much—just a little of the things That makes me a person feel human.

Dinkle wiggled across the sofa cushion to get closer and comfort Carly. *Maybe these poems represent a temporary circumstance in this woman's life.* Carly took a few sips of her lemonade and took out another folded and stapled few pages.

June 24, 1979—Sunday, 5:45 p.m.

I had Sara and Renee starting at 9:00 on Saturday morning. We went to the pool twice. We went to Roses, and I got them a gown, panties, flip-flops each. My emotions are so mixed up when I have them. I love my kids so much. They'll be grown before I know it.

August 6, 1979

Hi Sister, Hi Brother,

I hate to have to write to you instead of talk to you, but I guess it's better this way. Please don't take these letters home with you. I feel like if I don't talk to you sometimes, I'll die. I hope you know I love you and I never want you to think that I don't. I know daddy says things to influence the way you act, and I can see the fear in you when I see you. I feel so bad because I can't be with you. I am sending you two envelopes with stamps and my address on them. Please write me back. Tell me how you really feel. It is so important to me.

This is not an easy time for me or you but I'm hoping time will make things right. I haven't abandoned you. I want you to tell Sara and Renee every day how much I love them. I know they are confused. They just have to know how much I love them. I wish I could take you to the beach, but my car isn't good enough.

I care so much for all of you. Just hang in there and make the best of it. Allen says hello. He's good, kids. I'm as happy as I've ever been except for the fact that I can't see you. If you like living with your daddy, that's fine but I just wish he would let me, call you or come over or let you call me.

Be sure to tell Sara and Renee I love them. I love you too, you'll never know how much.

Mom

Carly wondered why the letter had been addressed to her sister and brother, yet it was talking to the children. And was Allen a new man in this woman's life? Carly put the papers on the table and just sat, not thinking, just trying to absorb and understand the feeling. She had kept a diary when she was younger. She had written some ideas, short stories, and even feelings she had experienced.

Never in her life could she imagine such feelings as expressed in these writings. She went outside and lay back in the reclining, cushioned lounge chair. Dinkle lay perched near the porch railings to keep guard. Sitting on her new porch was very relaxing compared to the apartment patio with the city noise and the activities of her neighbors. Carly's most vivid imagination could not fathom the life of the woman in the writings. The drizzling rain on the metal roof relaxed her and she drifted off to sleep.

She woke up from her brief nap and looked at her watch. Time for supper, but she didn't feel very hungry. Upon entering the back door, Carly noticed the answering machine light blinking and pressed the play button.

"Hello, Carly. I just got back into town. I sure have missed you. I'll call back in a little while or if you get this before then, just give me a ring. I love you. Talk to you soon."

Scott Matthews had returned from a bankers' convention in Raleigh. He had received his degree in business from UNC-Chapel Hill and returned to Lillington, where he now worked at the Harnett County Bank as a loan officer. Carly and Scott met two years prior at Doc Skinner's office. Dinkle was getting her puppy vaccinations and Tanner, Scott's three-year-old yellow lab was there for his rabies vaccination. Scott was six feet tall, slender build, with short, wavy light brown hair, and wore stylish clothes.

Carly took two oatmeal cookies from the cookie-tin and returned Scott's call. He answered. "Hi, Scott, sorry I missed your call. I was outside. I'm so glad you are back. How was your meeting in Raleigh?"

"Like the usual, lot of talk, pamphlets to review, rules and regulations of the banking commission. How is your move coming along? Have I missed out on all the hard labor?" he said hopefully.

"Don't worry. I saved a little work for you to do. No, really, it's coming along; I'm getting everything in place. I still have a few boxes to unpack, but it's livable. I really do like it."

"Can't wait to see it. How's Dinkle?"

"Just as sweet as ever. She's getting used to her new surroundings."

"I sure want to see you. I found something for you, I think you will like."

"What is it? Where did you get it?"

"You'll just have to be patient. You want to have lunch tomorrow? You're off work, right?"

"Yes. That sounds good. Do you want to meet at the *Green Hornet?*"

"Just the place I had in mind. I'll meet you there about 11:45."

"Don't forget my surprise," Carly quickly added.

"You want your surprise more than you want to see me? I'm so hurt."

"Oh Scott, you know I love surprises."

"And you know I love you, Carly, goodnight." Scott hung up.

Carly wouldn't allow herself to ponder long about love, her feelings for Scott, his feelings for her, nor what the future might bring.

She wanted to get to know more about the woman in the writings. *Maybe something in this box would be less depressing, maybe reveal a happy time or an expression of hope in the woman's life.* Carly pulled out a few of the stapled papers and an envelope. The front of the lavender-colored envelope read "*To my oldest daughter.*" Carly carefully unfolded the contents. *1970—over 40 years ago*, she said aloud.

11-12-70

My dearest daughter, this morning I feel compelled to write to you because as your mother I have said things that I did not mean. All this week I've had a weight on my chest. I'm hoping by being sincere to you, this will leave. I want you to know I'm the cause of my problems. Instead of helping you when you need it, it seems all I can do is help myself. When you have problems, it seems to throw me off balance. I know it does not seem that I love you, but I know I could not love anyone any more than I do you.

As far as the children, I've completely lost my heart to them. I am so sorry for saying I didn't want them over here (as I think back, I cannot believe that I could say a thing like that). I miss them so much, but I do not blame you for putting them in the nursery. I believe that I meant I did not want them all the time and that's not because I don't love them.

I know with all my heart I want you and your children to be happy. If I could take all you've been through off, you I would. It's this helpless feeling I get when I can't solve or help your problems. I don't know what's in this make-up of my mind that makes me say things I don't mean. Daddy reminded me yesterday I had always said more hurting remarks to him.

I'm thinking more seriously about my attitude and my problems. He also reminded me how bad it was to do something for someone and then throw it up to them. I'm so sorry for this and I can't explain why I do this. I know I do not feel this way until I get upset. I do wish I was blessed with a gentle attitude. I have really felt sorry for myself this week. I guess you being my child, it's a lot easier for me to know you do not mean some of the things you say when you are upset.

When the children did not come on Tuesday, I knew you believed what I had said. I hope in time you can forgive me for this. All I wanted to do was die and the helpless and alone feeling I had I did so want to just give up, but God and His mercy is helping me. I know God had kept his hand under you because I do not see how you've been through all you have unless His hand was there. I've got to believe that there will be a brighter day for you and the children.

What happens to Bruce you cannot help. You must do what you must do to help everyone concerned. If by chance he is sent to jail, he brought it on himself. God never intended for a man to hurt his wife, as Bruce has hurt you. I feel from the bottom of my heart you have got to think of what is best for the children and yourself.

I do not feel I can ever see them, and you go through this ever again. I know how I feel is beside the point, but it hurts so bad. I'm glad daddy has been able to help. I hope this letter explains a little how I feel. It's always been hard for me to say what I feel on paper. Please come when you can.

Love, Mother.

At first, Carly was confused but figured this letter was from the mother of the diary writer. Carly's mother had never said hurtful things that she could remember. Then she thought about her real mother, wondering what kind of person she might be. Of course, she would never know. She folded the letter and put it in the second box. She decided to read one more poem.

No More Struggling
When I was young, I jumped in a mud puddle to play.
Only to find it was quicksand.
I groped for a twig, a blade of grass, a rock, but always fell back in.
Then the limb came, to hope, security, peace, and calm.

The freedom I then knew was a huge stranger.
Guess what I did.
Went back to play in the old quicksand, forever. Not to struggle for freedom, but to let the limbs go by. Death is all that's left.

Carly had to take a break from reading. She could feel tears in her eyes. *How sad, who was this person, so forlorn, so hopeless feeling? What happened to her? Where is she now? She probably committed suicide.* She folded the letter and put it in the box.

In the kitchen, Carly made a small salad, buttered a couple of wheat crackers, and sat on a bar stool to eat her supper. *I wonder who the writer is, and where she is now. Is she alive?* Many questions filled her mind. Maybe Nellie would know something about the woman.

Carly went to the bathroom, filled the tub with hot water and bubbles of lavender and aloe. With candles lit, a classical music CD playing softly, and a glass of red wine, she would escape the writings for a while.

Dinkle sat at the doorway, on guard. Carly thought about her mother. Although Carly knew she was loved and had felt wanted all her life, her inner being wished for her real mom. She wondered where her real mom lived, what she did with her life, did she ever think about her baby. Carly didn't ever allow negative thoughts to come to the surface of her mind—thoughts like her mom didn't want her, or her mom had abandoned her in a bad way, or that her mom could even be dead.

The CD had started replay, the bath water had become lukewarm and Dinkle gave a little bark that said, time to go night-night.

Chapter Seven

Carly awoke feeling refreshed. She and Dinkle spent the early morning on the porch enjoying the cool country air. "You know, Dinkle, it's the time of year to plant flowers. I could make a little flower garden. Would you like that? Maybe even some rose bushes." Dinkle kept listening. "Next time I go to town, I will get a few tools and some pretty flower seeds to plant."

Carly enjoyed nurturing her houseplants, but now having a small yard, she wanted to try her green thumb outdoors.

Carly spent the rest of her morning unpacking the few remaining boxes, mostly books, which she placed on the wall bookcase in the hallway. She had a small collection of handmade pottery. Some pieces belonged to her mom who also collected pottery, beautiful, one-of-a-kind pieces. Carly liked to find new potters at street fairs and buy a piece of their work.

She took the pieces of pottery from the carton and placed each piece on the bookshelves along with her books, a photo of her parents at her college graduation, and a few other mementos. She hung her framed diploma, a portrait of her parents, and a collection of framed cross-stitched flowers over her desk. *Now, it really feels like home. I like it,* she thought.

Dinkle heard a car drive up in the driveway. Carly picked up her fearsome guard dog and opened the front door. A short, middle-aged woman conservatively dressed, her gray-streaked hair in a bun, stepped out of the car and walked up the driveway. "Good morning," Carly called out.

"Good morning to you. I don't want to bother you, but this is the first chance I've had to drop by and welcome you to the neighborhood."

The woman handed a foil-covered dish to Carly as she reached the front porch. With a warm, friendly smile, she said, "I'm Donna, Donna Brewer. I live in the next house down the road." She pointed in the direction.

"I am so happy to meet one of my neighbors, Donna. I'm Carly Jansen. This is Sunshine, we call her Dinkle."

"Such a cutie you are Sunshine Dinkle. Nice to meet you, Carly. I made this chocolate pie for you. Hope you like chocolate pie."

Carly opened the door. "Who doesn't like chocolate pie! Please, come in. You didn't have to go to all that trouble."

"No, I can't stay. I have a meeting at the church. I just wanted to say welcome to the neighborhood and let you know if you need anything, we're right down the road. Don't hesitate to call."

"I do thank you and you come back when you can visit longer."

"I will, and you have a nice day, Carly. Bye, Sunshine." Donna walked back to her car.

Carly took the pie to the kitchen. *One little piece will be OK.* She sliced a small piece of pie and placed it in one of her mother's China saucers, covered the pie, and put it in the refrigerator. The pie tasted just like her mom used to make. *Mom, I wish you were still here. I miss you and Dad so much.* She took a second bite of pie. Tears welled up in her eyes and overflowed. *Think of the good things. I had a good childhood and I have a good life now. Think about the future. Everything will be fine.* Carly rinsed her plate and fork. She looked at her watch, *less than two hours before I need to meet Scott.*

She went to the living room to learn more about the writer of the papers. Settling on the sofa, she picked out a small pink piece of paper and read:

12-11-79
Why do I always have to fight?
When I want—it's a struggle to have. I lose and I lose
No one agrees with my desires I wish I was in a cave.
So deep, so dark, so cold, so lonely. Nothing lasts or stays.
Allen is my only hope—
I'm tired—tired of having to convince Tired of fighting
It's Christmas—Be happy I will and if I'm not
I will fight not to show it.

Carly put the pink paper in the second box, picked out an envelope with "Mommie" written on the front, opened it, and read:

6-16-89

Mommie, Hey! How are you doing? Me and Renee are fine. Guess what, I passed. Now I am going to the eighth grade. Something happened to me last weekend. I almost got picked up by this 18-year-old guy. See daddy let me go to the beach with my best friend. Saturday night we went to this place that had a lot of rides. So, we rode some of the rides. Then at 11:00, we started back to the Substation where Cheri's parents dropped us off.

On our way back, Cheri went across a road without looking and she almost got hit. So, after that, these two guys came up and one of them stopped in front of me and the other stood behind me. Cheri just stood there. So, he told me how good I looked and to smile because I wasn't smiling. Then he told me to kiss him. I tried to make up all kinds of excuses. Then I told him to try it on Cheri. So, he turned around and I stepped over to the left and ran and I took Cheri with me. So that is the end of my story.

Well, I guess I don't have anything to say but I love you! I love you! Please write back soon.

Love, Sara, and Renee

Carly thought, *1978, 1979, and now 1989.* She picked up the journal books out of the box and opened each one to check the date. *I need to see if there is a beginning. Where does it all begin?* There were various dates from 1976, 1979, 1980, 1981, 1983, 1982, and 1985. Most of the journals contained writing only on the first several pages, and then they were blank. Placing each journal in date order, 1979 was the earliest, so she started with that one.

October 4, 1979

Dear Parents

I'm going to try to be just as open and honest in this letter as I possibly can.

I know for a fact that I have suffered emotionally for a long time. I have had different circumstances than anyone else in the family. I suffer from feelings of inadequacy, loneliness, not being accepted, difference, and more. First, I would like for you to know that I wish I could have the kind of open communication relationship with you that other people have. It seems I've always had to be what was expected, even though I'm loved, I'm not accepted. I'm not talking about approval, but acceptance. I stay depressed. Sometimes I'm able to rise above it by not giving a damn.

When I go to see you, we talk "weather" talk. When I try to tell you other things, I may as well be talking to the wall. I'm a good person inside. I can't take many more months or years like I've had since 1966. I'm scared of love because it has always been so conditional. It seems when I need people most, they go away.

I accept you both the way you are. I wish you would me. I am very bitter inside about lots of things in life. One of them is religion, church, or whatever name you want to put on it. If you need it, fine. It's never done me any good so I would appreciate it very much if you wouldn't try to witness to me or get me to go to church. I have very strong opinions on the subject. Experience got me to this point and experience will have to change it if it ever changes.

I guess this is a dumb letter to be writing but I just needed to tell you how I really feel. Now either accept me as I am or forever leave me alone.

I don't need no shrink or no daggum preacher. All I've ever needed is a family.

I just think it's sad to be 29-1/2 years old and never really had a heart-to-heart, open, unconditional talk with my parents.

Love and regrets,
Your little black sheep daughter.

Carly had extreme difficulty relating to the feelings expressed by this woman to her parents. It was as if she were reading a book or watching a movie. Carly thought, *if the writer was almost 30 in 1979; that would make her around 65 years old now. She's probably dead by now. I'll talk with Nellie and try to get a little information and history about the woman who had previously lived here.*

She turned the page in the journal but looking at her watch, Carly realized time had passed so fast. She reluctantly placed the journal on the table. She wanted to read all day, but instead freshened up, changed into a button-up white cotton blouse and jeans, quickly brushed through her hair, and went to meet Scott for lunch.

In the car, she fumbled in her purse for her ringing cell phone. "Hello."

"Hey, Carly. I tried the house but figured you must have left. I'm so sorry, but I can't make it for lunch. The boss has called a meeting."

"Oh, that's too bad." Carly was surprised by the lack of disappointment she expressed.

"I'll give you a call later today after I get out of the meeting."

"OK. No problem, I'll just get a bite of lunch and visit with Nellie."

"Tell her I said hello."

"I will. I guess this means I won't get my surprise," Carly said with true disappointment.

"I might keep it until Christmas," Scott kidded. "I love you. Talk to you later."

"Bye, Scott." *I could have stayed home and read some more of the diary. Oh well, a break might be good.*

Nellie greeted Carly when she entered the diner as if she hadn't seen her in a long time. "Hey there, my girl! Come on in and take a seat. The usual?"

Nellie made the usual, garden salad with oil and vinegar dressing, a glass of unsweetened tea, and brought it to her table. The lunch crowd had not yet arrived. "Surprised to see you today. Thought it would be tomorrow."

"Well, Scott was going to meet me here, but his boss called a meeting at the last minute, so he couldn't make it."

Nellie took a seat at the table. "You know, I believe that young man is going to ask you to marry him soon."

Carly almost choking on her salad, "What? What makes you think that?"

"Ya'll have been seeing each other for how long now, about a year or two?"

"Yeah, about two years, I can't believe it's been that long."

"If he does propose, what are you going to say?" Nellie asked.

"I might make him wait for an answer like he makes me wait for surprises."

"Surprises?" Nellie questioned.

"Yes, he said he had me a surprise, something he bought on his trip to Raleigh. When he had to cancel lunch, I made a comment about not getting my surprise and he said he was going to keep it until Christmas."

"I bet it's an engagement ring," Nellie guessed.

A few construction workers entered the door and Nellie resumed her role as hostess and waitress.

Carly had been so busy with her career, the loss of her parents, and the move, she had little time for romantic thoughts. She was not sure what her answer to a proposal would be. She finished her lunch, paid Nellie the cashier. "Thanks a lot, Nellie. It was good as always. I'll probably see you tomorrow."

"OK, sweetie, you take care. Give Dinkle a hug for me."

Chapter Eight

Instead of going home, Carly decided to go by the nursery to buy flowers for her new garden. They had so many flowers that were already blooming that she decided on those rather than seeds. She could enjoy them sooner. Her backyard had a nice morning sun, as well as a shady area near the edge of the woods. She got some advice from the nursery employee about the best kind of flowers to get. She picked out various shades of impatiens that do well in the sun or shade and purchased a couple of needed hand tools.

When she arrived home, Dinkle was waiting by the front door. With her hands full, Carly couldn't give Dinkle her usual rub on the head.

"I bought us some flowers to plant, Dinkle, impatiens, red ones, pink and white ones. The man at the nursery recommended them," she said to Dinkle as she took the tray of plants to the back porch. Dinkle turned into a bloodhound once again, but only briefly. "You can help me plant them this weekend, Dinkle." Dinkle barked in agreement.

In the kitchen, Carly put the teakettle on the stove and then went to the bedroom to change into her shorts and tank top. *What will my answer be if Scott asks me to marry him? I wonder if he did buy me a ring. Oh, well, I'll know soon.* Carly went back to the kitchen, refreshed Dink's water, and food, made herself tea, picked out a couple of journals from the box that she had left on the coffee table, and went outside to sit on the porch to read more.

She opened the first journal to the marker she had placed.

October 22, 1979, 12:00 midnight
I'm in my room I rented from a retired schoolteacher, Ms. Kelly. Sometimes I wonder what I want in life. I'm almost 30 years old and now I have nothing I had six months ago. I hope I get that loan tomorrow. I want to get financially secure, and I've got the kids this weekend and I'm broke.
I love to write in this book. I can write anything I feel.

Carly guessed the writer must have four children, but not have them with her, and she had mentioned a man named Bruce and a man named Allen.

Bruce, her former husband and the children's father, and Allen must be her new love.

Oct 26, 1979, Friday, 9:00 p.m.
Here I am, where I'll be all my life—ALONE.
I went to see Mommie in the hospital tonight. There is still a gap between us. Boy, there is a big one between me and Daddy. I was hoping daddy would come and see my room but no—it seems everyone has gone. I got my room and I got Ms. Kelly.
I guess, I'll fix me a cup of coffee. My head is hurting. My kids—that subject will always hurt. I love them so much. I wish it was different.

November 12, 1979

Melanie, Jeremy, Sara, Renee
I love you so much. There isn't a minute in the day that I don't think about all of you. I worry about how all this mess is affecting you. It tears my heart out when Sara cries.
I'm glad you have an apartment now. I hope daddy will pay the bills right so you can stay there.
I hope when you get older you will understand why I have had to do the things I have. If you ever need me, call me. I'll do anything for you. You can tell me anything.
I'll write you a letter at least once a week, so you should get one; if not, your daddy is keeping them from you. If you'll write me back in these stamped envelopes and tell me everything about things. If you ever find an address, I can send mail to, so daddy won't see it, let me know. Always know I love you and would help you in anything. I'm your mother, I understand, and I care.
If you get a chance, call me. I won't be seeing you probably for a good while. Daddy isn't thinking about you, just hurting me. I don't want to get you in trouble with him. Tell Sara and Renee every day that I love them. I know they won't understand the reason I have to not seen them for a while.
Be good, send me pictures if you can. Please write. I never want to hurt you. I always want to understand. I love you very much. I must fight all the sadness I feel. No one knows how my heart hurts. Let me know something very special all of you would like from me for Christmas.

Listen to the words of "If You Remember Me" on G105 by Kris Thompson.

Warm tears formed in Carly's eyes. *Oh, my goodness, could this be real?* Her mind could not imagine all the turmoil and heartache for this woman and her children. What had happened? She got up to go back inside. The phone was ringing. She had difficulty controlling her emotions. She realized that the diary was affecting how she felt. Her life seemed so superficial and frivolous when compared to the life of the diary writer. "Hello."

"Hey Carly, sorry about lunch today."

"No problem. How was your meeting?" Carly asked, as usual. "It was mainly to discuss some changes in policy regarding loan applications and go over some highlights from the conference last week."

"Sounds like you would have had more fun having lunch with me."

"I'm sure. How's Nellie and the gang?"

"Nellie's always the same, works her butt off. She should really own the place because without her, there would not even be a diner. We were able to visit a little while before the lunch crowd came in. When I left the diner, I went to Lillington and bought some flowers for my yard. I think I will plant them in the front yard and backyard, you know, make a little flower garden this weekend."

Carly knew Scott didn't care much for yard work. He would rather use his fingers on a calculator.

"Would you be interested in a steak dinner tomorrow night, baked potato, salad, and all the trimmings?" Scott asked.

"You buy and I'll cook." Although Scott could cook, Carly preferred her way of seasoning food. "A bottle of red wine would be nice."

"You got it. I'll go by dad's place after work and pick up a couple of thick-cut T-bones and be at your place shortly after six." Scott's father owned Womble's Meat Market. Carly's dad had worked there as a young man before he married.

Carly was hoping to get more time to read the journals after work but couldn't neglect everything in life. "I'll see you then. Oh, Scott—"

"Yes?"

"Don't forget my surprise," Carly jokingly ordered. "Goodnight, my impatient love. See you tomorrow."

Chapter Nine

Saturday morning, Carly awoke with a dull headache. A little too much wine, she thought. She passed the bookshelf in the hall and admired the miniature, handmade pottery vase that Scott had bought for her at an art festival in Cary and had finally given to her after dinner last night. *I guess the proposal will come later. Nellie will be disappointed.*

She went to the bathroom, took an aspirin for her headache. The only thing she could think about was the woman in the journal. She would be able to read a lot more this weekend since Scott was going to be with some of his college friends who were coming to town.

Dinkle sat beside her food bowl in the kitchen. "Are you hungry, sweetie? Let me get you some breakfast." She put *Alpo Filet Mignon* in the food bowl. Carly was still full since last night's supper but toasted a slice of wheat toast, fixed a cup of green tea. "We're going to make a flower garden today, Dinkle."

Carly picked up the phone, dialed the *Green Hornet Grill*. "Green Hornet, how can I help you?" Nellie answered.

"Hey Nellie, it's me, Carly."

"Good morning, Carly. Is something wrong?" It was unusual for Carly to call Nellie at work, and so early on Saturday.

"No, nothing's wrong. I was just wondering what time you get off today and if you had any plans?"

"Like usual, we'll close the grill after lunch, around 1:00 and, no, don't have anything planned. Did Scott ask you the big question?"

"No, I'm afraid not."

"Well, what was his surprise?"

"He bought me a handmade miniature pottery vase at a street arts festival in Cary. It's very pretty. Anyway, the reason I called is I was wondering if you would like to spend the afternoon with me. I'm going to make a little flower garden. Maybe we could go to the flea market in Angier or Dunn."

"Now you know you got me hooked." The bell on the diner door rang. "Ya'll come on in. I'll be with you in a minute." Nellie called out to the customers.

"I know you're busy, Nellie. I'll see you this afternoon."

"OK, see you then."

The toast had not been enough breakfast, so Carly fixed herself a bowl of bran and nuts cereal with slices of banana, covered with 1% milk. The TV weather forecaster said the humidity would be low for the weekend with cooler-than-normal temperatures.

Thinking aloud, Carly said, "You know, Dinkle, since I'm going to wait for Nellie before planting the flowers, I can read more writings from the box this morning." She rinsed her dishes and then curled up on the sofa to continue her reading.

November 13, 1979

Dear Melanie and Jeremy,

I would like for you to send me some pictures sometime. I would love a school picture. Also, if you would let me know a couple of things you really want for Christmas and Sara and Renee? I'll write you very often.

Also, I'll send you your Christmas presents. I'm sorry I can't see you, but I can't keep facing the problems your daddy gives me. I want you to know I love all of you and if you need me, call me. I can't stand to see Sara cry. I can't even see you for five minutes without your daddy being stupid. I'm sorry it has to be this way. If you need me or want to talk, call, or write. Unless you call or write, I won't hear from you for a long time. Tell Sara and Renee, I love them every day.

Love always, Mommie. (Mailed 11-14-79)

Carly wondered if the children really received this letter or did their dad hid it from them.

After reading several more entries from November 1979, mostly repeating the same words, Carly laid the journal gently on her lap. She felt numb, almost trance-like. She did not know what to feel. She sat there for quite some time, just trying to imagine, to understand what she was reading. The utter and complete loneliness and confusion this woman felt was so foreign to Carly. Some of the letters had notations of the dates they were mailed, and she wondered if the children ever received them.

Dinkle jumped off the sofa and brought Carly out of her thoughts. She sighed deeply and lifted the journal. The rest of that book was empty.

Carly reached into the second box to find the date on the letter she had read. *1989, ten years—this woman had been away from her children for at least ten years? What had happened? I have to find out who lived here. Maybe one of her children lived here and had the box. The woman could be in an institution, or even dead. Such pain and desperation, she may have committed suicide.*

For the first time in a long time, Carly wanted some junk food, a big banana split, a bag of chips, and ranch dip. She went to the kitchen, got a few stalks of celery from the refrigerator instead, and returned to the sofa. The first entry in the next journal had no date but must have been in January 1980 because of the entries that followed.

Carly scanned most of the entries as they were more of the same feelings of depression and loneliness. In college, Carly had taken psychology courses. Why didn't this woman get help, counseling, or something? She is definitely very sick, emotionally for sure, maybe mentally as well. Maybe that's why she doesn't have her children. Carly turned back to the diary but after a couple of pages, she laid the journal on the table.

Carly sat quietly, stroking Dinkle softly. "Thank you, God, for my life," she spoke aloud. She looked down at her sweet pet, "Enough for now, Dinkle. I am going to plant some flowers. Are you ready to play outside?"

Dinkle followed Carly to the bedroom. She changed into a pair of shorts and a T-shirt, socks, and tennis shoes. Carly went to the back porch, gathered the hand tools and the flat of impatiens. "Come on, Dinkle. You stay close to me, don't go running away." With Dinkle right on her heels, they went to the front yard. Carly stood in the yard and looked around. "Now I wonder where the best place would be to have a flower garden."

Dinkle didn't have an opinion. "You know, I think it would be better in the backyard, near the porch, where we can enjoy them when we sit outside." Dinkle followed her back around the house to the backyard. Carly loosened the soil, pulled the grass and weeds out of the small area along the front edge of the porch. She dug the holes and put the plants in each, just as the man at the nursery had told her, and patted the ground around the base while Dinkle lay in the grass, taking it all in. Carly went inside, filled a pitcher with water, and returned to water each plant.

Carly stepped back and admired her accomplishment. She couldn't wait to show Nellie what a gardener she had turned out to be. Now if they just stay alive, she thought. She put her tools back on the porch and went inside to straighten the house a bit before Nellie arrived. The phone rang. "Hello."

"I'm getting ready to leave the diner shortly. I have some chicken salad, freshly made this morning, that I'll bring for our lunch. Do you have any lettuce?"

"Nellie, you don't have to do that, but it does sound good and yes, I have spinach, not lettuce."

"That'll work. I'll see you as soon as I get closed up around here." Carly set two plates with silverware on the tablemats along with two glasses and napkins. She tidied the living room and slid the boxes to the far side of the sofa. *Maybe Nellie knows who used to live here.*

Chapter Ten

Nellie admired Carly's new flower garden. After lunch, Carly showed her pottery collection to Nellie, explaining a little history of each piece. "My mom gave me this little vase for my sixteenth birthday. It's probably my favorite. This miniature vase is the one that Scott got for me when he was on his business trip last week."

After a few more show-and-tell items, the two women decided to sit in the living room, where it was cool.

"You know, Carly, I've been thinking about asking you this for a while and I hope it doesn't upset you, but have you ever thought about trying to find your birth mother?"

"I have wondered about her, who she is, where she is, what kind of person she might be, but I never wanted to hurt my mom, my adoptive mom."

"Did your mom ever tell you anything about your birth mother?"

"Not that I can remember. It seems I knew very early in life that I had been adopted. My parents made me feel wanted and loved in a very special way. I could never do anything that would hurt them."

"I can understand that Carly, but what about now?"

"To tell you the truth, I'm a little scared to find my birth mother. What if she still doesn't want to have anything to do with me?"

"That is one possibility. You would need to prepare yourself for almost anything."

"I guess I'll think about it some more. Besides, I wouldn't even know where to begin searching for her."

"Where were you born?"

"My birth certificate says I was born in Harnett County to Paul and Helen Jansen. My real birth certificate can never be released. The records are sealed forever. That's the law, at least in North Carolina."

"Do you know that to be a fact, Carly?"

"I'm pretty sure."

"Let me see what I can find out, and you keep thinking about it and we'll discuss it again. Is that OK with you?"

"Of course, it's fine with me." Carly could not believe that she would ever know her birth mother, but inside she had a twinge of excitement over the possibility. She then thought about the mother in the writings. "Changing the subject, Nellie, did you ever know anyone who lived in this house?"

"No, can't say I did. Most of the folks that come to the diner are from Lillington. Why do you ask?"

Carly wanted to tell Nellie about the box but decided maybe a later time would be better. "Just wondering about it, that's all."

Dinkle made her entrance into the room, bringing her stuffed toy with her, and jumped up on the sofa with Carly.

"Nellie, do you still want to go to the flea market?"

"You know, I believe I'd rather wait until it is a little cooler. I've enjoyed our lunch and our talk. I had better be going, though. I know you have things you want to do, and I have places to go and people to see."

Carly picked up Dinkle with her stuffed toy and walked Nellie to the door. "I understand. We can go to the flea market another time, hopefully soon."

They stood on the porch and Carly waved Dinkle's paw bye-bye to Nellie as she left.

Chapter Eleven

That afternoon Carly decided she would do a little more organizing of her home office area. She turned on the radio to a jazz station and, with Dinkle faithfully sitting at the doorway guarding the office. She began sorting through her files and records. Her desk set beside the window.

Directly in front of the window were her shelves of various houseplants where the morning light would come through. The chore of sorting through her files occupied her thoughts for much of the afternoon. After most of the files were put away and her reference books on journalism were on the shelf, she decided to call it a day. Dinkle could read her mind and got up to lead Carly out of the office.

In the kitchen, she turned on the evening news and started making her favorite artichoke salad with Caesar dressing, while the pork chop baked in the toaster oven. She sat at the bar and ate her supper while she watched the national news. She did not pay attention to the news closely. Her thoughts were on the writings in the box as well as the possibility of finding her real parents.

When finished with supper, she rinsed her dishes, turned off the television, and resumed her place on the sofa. She knew Scott was spending the weekend with his friends, so he would not be calling. She continued reading the diary from 1980. The next entry was dated April 23, 1980, a letter to the four children that reiterated the same feelings as expressed previously. It was signed, "*I love you all the way up to the sky, Love Mommie.*"

June 6, 1980, 10:30 a.m.
Allen and I married 5/21/80 at 2:05 p.m.—

Carly was surprised. She had been reading the entries in chronological order but there had only been one mention of Allen.

9-16-80
Hell! That's what it is! Sometimes I ache and hurt so bad. Just to touch or see or hold my kids. I called Sara at her grandma's house. She told me that

she had just got a spanking for telling a fib. I don't think I could live if this feeling stayed or if it got worse. I want to hold Sara so bad. I'm missing all her childhood. I don't even know Renee anymore. Jeremy is like a stranger. I miss so much talking to them, watching them. Even their arguing.

My plane has no landing gear This I didn't foresee.

I could feel the fear of take-off.

The beauty and excitement of flight and dream of a wonderful destiny. But I can't touch down.

My plane has no landing gear. Sometimes I see the fuel nearing empty. I am only seeing now the crash.

I've got myself padded

With money, companions, work, playtimes, etc. They will be of naught when F turns to E.

Carly stopped reading and just stared at the page. This woman had a creative side, a way to express herself abstractly. She was different that anyone Carly had ever known. It sounded like the woman was losing her mind. She reached for another folded piece of paper.

10-28-80

Dear parents of mine:

As of today, it has been three weeks since I have heard from you. I have decided not to ever call you again or go over. You know all my phone numbers and you know where I live. If I am not just like you want me to be or talk or think like you want me to you leave me alone until "I come to my senses" or you leave me "in God's hands."

Well, in my opinion, the lack of your hands and the control of God's hands put me where I am right now. That was cruel, wasn't it? I, like you, have a lot of things on my mind and some things worry me bad. I am self-sufficient because I have always had to be. I have always had to have so much responsibility and so has Melanie.

Sometimes I just wish I had my kids and lived far away. My kids being away from me hurts so much. You will never see this letter or probably never know how I really feel. There isn't anyone who can take your parents' place. I worry about you both. I still say out of the whole family I don't belong.

Everyone is in the family but me. Now that I really want my kids to know they have a mother, they aren't with me enough to even know me, much less how I really am. I have changed but I resent the fact that you both judge me so badly.

I really get to the place I don't care about anything; the only thing I must do is fight depression, so I won't stop caring about myself to the point of not wanting to live. I am good, I am honest, I am dependable, I am loving, I am tender, I am understanding, but the truth is, who gives a damn! I will survive and the only one in the whole world who ever really loved me is Nannie.

You know she never said to my recollection that she loved me, but she always showed it. I have had so many people tell me they love me, but they don't show it. I'm the world's worst person when it comes to showing love. Maybe because I don't know how—I don't say it because to me that is of no use. Maybe even worse than that, I don't know how to accept love because I don't think I have ever realized that I have had it. I'm glad I'm a survivor but I really wish I didn't have to be. I love you both and I wish life could have been different for us.

It really makes me sad when I see grown people who have a good relationship with their parents. I know I will never have that because I am not the way you want me to be, but I am me and I hope I always have the capacity to be me.

Carly thought about her real mom. Maybe I just need to leave well enough alone. Finding my real parents may open a new life that is bad. Again, she thanked God for giving her such wonderful and loving adoptive parents.

Dec. 19, 1980, 1:30

Last night was hard on my emotions, all I could think of was my kids. I really don't have anyone to talk to. Christmas used to be so happy with the kids around to talk to and get excited with. This is the second Christmas without them. When I think I've almost missed two years of their life! Sara's birthday is on the 31st. I think of all the nights I haven't put them to bed or bathed them or held them. I hurt so bad. I want them so bad. I've got to wait until after Christmas to have them. I'm scared they don't think I care or want them. Life feels so lonely. I wish I wasn't alive sometimes. Loneliness is awful. No one to talk to at all about anything but weather or surface things. I really need someone so bad to listen.

Melanie, Jeremy, Renee, and Sara, I love you with all my heart. You, I hope, will never know the pain I feel. I don't know what to get you for Christmas. I feel like nothing is enough for you to show you. I guess I should look on the good side. I miss you and love you so much. Just please know, I think in time things will work out. I love you all so much. Mommie.

12-31-80 5:35
Today is Sara's birthday.

Having finished the diary from 1980, Carly knew she had to take a break from all of this. It was beginning to affect her mood. She closed the two boxes and carried them to her office. She could read more another day. She really wanted to find out who the woman was who had lived such a horrible life and where she was now. Where were the children?

Chapter Twelve

When Carly left the newspaper office at noon on Monday, she walked two blocks to the realtor's office where Mr. Baker had worked for as long as Carly could remember. As she entered, the receptionist greeted her in a friendly manner. Mr. Baker was coming out of his office and when he saw Carly, he put on his huge salesman smile. "Why Carly! How in the world are you? It's been a while. You know I have been meaning to come by and see how the house is working out for you, but you know, I get busy and all."

"The house is feeling more like a home every day, Mr. Baker," Carly said.

"I'm so glad, Carly. Now, what can I do for you?" He turned to the receptionist and said, "Sally, please call the Dunnavans and tell them I am running a few minutes late." Mr. Baker motioned for Carly to step inside his office. "Have a seat, Carly. Would you like some coffee or a Pepsi?"

"No, thank you. I just came to ask you a question. I don't want to take up a lot of your time," Carly said as she sat down. She continued, "I wanted to ask you about the people who lived in my house before I bought it. Do you happen to remember their name or anything about them?"

"No, don't recall. Mr. O'Neal owned that house, and he was the one renting it out. When he died, his sons put it up for sale and that's how I obtained ownership." Mr. Baker said.

"Oh, I understand," said Carly.

"You know, I believe the man's name who rented it was Josh. I can't remember where I heard it. Maybe Ms. Maggie knows something more about him," he suggested.

Carly reached into her purse and got a notepad and pen and wrote the name Josh. Carly was disappointed. Surely someone would know more about them. "Thanks so much, Mr. Baker. I appreciate your time. I know you have an appointment."

"Any time Carly. Don't be a stranger and if you know of anyone interested in buying a house, or selling, hope you'll tell them to give me a call."

"Of course, I will. Goodbye, Mr. Baker, and thanks again."

On the way back to her car, Carly stopped by the drugstore to pick up a few things. The bell rang as the door opened and Ms. Maggie greeted her. "Come in, Carly. How are you?"

"Very well, thank you." Carly got a couple of needed items and when she came back to the checkout, she saw that there were no other customers in the drugstore and decided to ask Ms. Maggie about the previous renters. "Ms. Maggie, I was wondering, did you know who was living in my house before me? Mr. Baker said he thought the man's name was Josh."

Ms. Maggie furrowed her brow in thought. "Well, yes, seems like I do remember him, sort of artist-type looking fellow, or a woodsman, don't know, but he did come in every so often. Not real talkative though." Ms. Maggie punched the numbers on the old cash register and handed the receipt to Carly. "Why are you asking?"

"No reason, just curious." Picking up her shopping bag, she asked, "Do you know if the man was married?"

"I don't think so. I did see a woman with him occasionally when he came to town. I don't recall ever hearing her name, though. They seemed like the type to keep to themselves mostly."

"Well, thanks very much, Ms. Maggie. You have a good day."

As Carly opened the door, Ms. Maggie called back to her. "You know, Carly, I believe she was the woman in that wreck back a few years, the one where that pregnant lady was killed."

Carly almost dropped her bag. She closed the door and went back to the register. "She was the one killed?"

"No, she was the woman driving the other car," Ms. Maggie answered. "Come to think of it, I believe she must have moved shortly after the wreck because she never came to town, only Josh."

"I saw an article about that in the archives when I first started working at the newspaper. That was awful. It didn't give any names, however."

"Oh yes, it was very sad. I believe the lady that was killed was from Dunn. Poor thing and she was pregnant too. That's all people talked about for the longest time. You know they finally put up a four-way stop at that intersection but what if really needs, if you ask me, is a stoplight."

"I really appreciate the information, Ms. Maggie. I'll see you later."

After leaving the drugstore, Carly greeted a few people on the street and when she got to her car, she decided she would stop by the diner on the way home.

Nellie was glad to see her, as always. "Are you having your usual today?" she asked.

"No thanks, Nellie. I believe I would just like a cup of that good coffee you make."

"Just made some, in fact, so it will be nice and fresh." She poured the coffee. "I'm glad you stopped by. I've been looking into how you go about finding biological parents and it was rather complicated to be truthful. Everybody says those files are closed and sealed and the law won't allow anyone to find out the information. But I did find a private investigator who does it for a fee."

Carly didn't know what to say. She sipped her coffee. "Um, good coffee, just what I needed. You sure don't waste time, Nellie. How much is the fee?"

"Oh, don't worry yourself about that. I just want to know if you have thought any more about it and if you want to pursue it."

Carly sat her cup down and looked at Nellie. "You know, Nellie, my life has been very good. I also realize there is a huge range of possibilities that can come from this search, from fantastic to disastrous. I can't tell if I am excited or scared about the possibility."

"I know, honey. It's a big step. If you'd like, I can have the detective contact you about the process, you know, to ease your mind about how it works and what to expect."

"That would be good. I need to know more about what they do."

"You don't have to worry, my girl; I will be with you through it, no matter what the outcome. You understand that, don't you?"

"Yes, Nellie, you are such a good friend."

Nellie added coffee to Carly's cup. "Well, how are things with you and Scott these days?"

"About the same. He's busy with his work and his friends. We talk on the phone almost every day. I haven't minded too much though because I am enjoying doing things around my house." Carly opened her purse, took out the money, and left it on the counter. "I better be going, Nellie." She decided not to talk to Nellie about the information Ms. Maggie had told her.

"I'll call the agency and give them your phone number, OK?"

"That will be fine. I'll talk to you later," Carly said as she left the diner.

Chapter Thirteen

The detective was coming to Carly's this afternoon. Carly was feeling anxious. Hopefully, talking to the investigator will help. Was she ready for what might happen? The doorbell rang and Dink followed Carly to the door. Thinking it was the man from the agency, she opened the door and was surprised to see Nellie.

"Hey, Nellie. Is everything OK? Who's minding the store?"

"I knew the detective was coming and I wouldn't think of not being here with you, my dear. Ed's taking care of things. I told him I wouldn't be gone too long and besides, the lunch crowd has come and gone."

Before Carly could close the door, a newer model white Toyota Camry pulled into the driveway. Carly had expected an older, overweight, balding man, an image that must have come from watching television. Carly was pleasantly surprised.

Thorne Davenport walked up to the porch and Carly found herself holding her breath. He carried himself with much confidence. "Good afternoon. Carly?"

"Yes, I'm Carly. You must be Mr. Davenport."

"Call me Thorne, please."

"Come in, Thorne. This is my friend, Nellie; she's the one who contacted your agency."

"Glad to make your acquaintance, Nellie."

"Please, come into the living room. Would you like coffee or lemonade?" Nellie and Thorne both declined. They all sat down, Nellie in her favorite chair, Carly and Thorne on the sofa.

Thorne handed an information brochure about his agency to Carly and Nellie. He explained the process and other pertinent information.

"How long does it take?" Carly asked.

Thorne cleared his throat. "It varies. Sometimes as little as a couple of weeks, sometimes it may take a few months."

"If you find my mother, what then? Do you bring her here, or do I go to her?"

"The contact between you will be of mutual agreement. I will supply you with the name and whereabouts of your biological mother and it is up to you to contact her and go from there."

Carly felt more at ease. She liked Thorne and felt she could trust him. "So, how do we get started?"

"Your friend, Nellie, has taken care of the financial matters. I just have to ask you a few questions and get you to sign the agreement."

"I have no real information, only my adoptive birth certificate. I have no idea of where you would start looking."

"That's my job," Thorne reassured her.

Carly read and signed the simple agreement. It was mainly describing the legalities protecting the agency against any claims, and that the fee had been paid.

After Thorne left, Carly and Nellie speculated on the outcome.

All kinds of situations were possible.

Nellie said, "Let's just see what happens. Take it one step at a time. You just know I'm here for you, Carly. All you need to do is pick up the phone or come by the diner. OK, sweetie?"

"Oh Nellie, I don't know how to thank you. I hope it all turns out good."

"Me too. Now, I need to get back before Ed has a conniption. He hasn't had the full responsibility in quite some time. See you later. Call me if you hear anything."

"I will," Carly replied. She closed the door and went to the kitchen to make chamomile tea. She gave Dinkle a treat and together they went to the living room. Carly's mind was spinning, so many thoughts all jumbled on top of one another. She lay her head on the throw pillow, pulled the knitted Afghan over her, and drifted off to sleep. The ringing of the phone jolted her awake.

"Hello."

"What are you doing?" Scott asked.

"Oh, I just made a cup of tea and was relaxing. Where are you?"

"I'm getting ready to leave work. How about Chinese, my treat?"

Although Carly wasn't really in the mood, she thought the distraction might be helpful. "Sounds good. What time?"

"Say, about an hour."

"Fine, see you then."

She freshened up a bit, changed into clean jeans and a teal-colored cotton shirt. *I wonder if I should tell Scott. Of course, I do. Why wouldn't I tell him that I'm going to try to find my real mom? He will probably be happy for me. Anyway, too late to turn back now.*

Scott arrived with the food. Carly had the table set up and the tea made. They talked about things in general, mostly about Scott's work. After they finished supper, Carly thought it would be nice to sit outside. She had difficulty concentrating on their conversation because all she could think about was how to tell him her news. They sat quietly, and finally, Carly spoke up. "I had something interesting happen today."

"Oh yeah, tell me about it. Something good?"

"That remains to be seen. Anyway, a while back, Nellie asked me if I had ever thought about finding my biological parents." Carly saw Scott's facial expression change.

"I hope you said no."

"Not exactly. I said I would think about it."

"And then you said no, right?"

"Why do you say that?"

"Because Carly, you should let the past stay in the past. No good will come of it. Why would you want to mess up everything? You have everything going for you. Besides, have you thought about how bad things could turn out for you?"

Carly was taken aback by his remarks. She hadn't even told him any details and he was already putting a negative spin on it. She hesitated.

"Well, what happened?" Scott seemed a little irritated.

"Nothing yet. The private investigator came by today and talked with me. So, the process has started. You know, it could turn out good."

"I don't know how." Scott gulped the last swallow of his tea. "Listen, I better get going. I have to be at my best tomorrow, we have an early meeting."

"Scott, don't be like this. Can't you try to understand? Won't you at least let me tell—" Carly stopped talking. She could see that Scott was not interested. They quietly walked back into the house, but Scott continued to the front door.

"I'll give you a call tomorrow, Carly."

She felt like hollering back *don't bother but* said nothing.

Carly didn't sleep very well that night. Her thoughts were reeling from the day. She was glad she didn't have to go to work the next day. Maybe she would start a small vegetable garden.

Chapter Fourteen

Around 9:00 the next morning, Carly's phone rang. "Hello."

"Good morning, hope I didn't get you out of bed."

Recognizing her boss' voice, she said, "Oh no. Good morning to you, Mr. Bennett."

"Carly, I realize that you've wanted a special project, more in the field of journalism. So, I've been giving it some consideration."

"That sounds great. Do you want me to come to the office?"

"No, that's not necessary. I'll just give you the idea and let you go with it, however, you think best."

"That sounds fine." Carly felt her pulse increasing. She had no idea that she would be offered this kind of opportunity this soon.

"I think it would be of interest to our readers if we ran a series on the history of our city, maybe even the surrounding communities. Would you be interested in doing something like that? I was thinking maybe a weekly article for a month or so. What do you think, Carly?"

"I would like it very much. I'll need to do quite a bit of research. When do you want it to begin running in the paper?"

"No real hurry. Just keep me informed on your progress and we'll make further decisions along the way."

"OK, Mr. Bennett. I really appreciate this opportunity. I'll get started on it right away."

"You're welcome, Carly, and I'm sure you will do a good job. Talk to you soon."

Carly jumped up and down with excitement. Dinkle started barking as if he were celebrating with her. "Oh Dinkle, I'm going to write an article, and not one, but many. I can't believe it! I have to get to the library." She stopped and thought, slow down, my goodness. On the way down the hall to her office, she sang aloud, "I'm going to be a journalist, a journalist, a journalist; I'm going to be a journalist, yes I am!"

She took out a notepad and noted some initial ideas to include in the articles. Then she showered and dressed.

Carly started out for the library, but since it was lunchtime, she stopped by the diner, excited to tell Nellie the good news of her assignment. As she neared the diner, she saw a police car and an ambulance in the parking lot, lights flashing. *Oh no, oh my, not Nellie. Oh God, please not Nellie.*

She pulled to the side of the parking lot, not to interfere with the situation. As she was running to the door, Nellie walked out the door, crying, wiping her eyes with a tissue. Carly called out. "Nellie, Nellie, are you alright? What's happened?"

Nellie could hardly speak. "Oh, my dear, it's Ed. I think he's had a heart attack. What am I going to do?"

Carly tried in vain to comfort Nellie. The ambulance took Ed away, but by the time Nellie and Carly arrived at Good Hope Hospital, Ed had passed.

The diner was closed for that weekend. Ed's funeral was held on Sunday, a simple service, and many of the town's people came in support of Nellie and to give her their condolences.

Chapter Fifteen

On Monday of the following week, Carly went to the diner to help Nellie clean up and get things in order. Carly had put her assignment on the back burner for a bit. She knew Mr. Bennett would certainly understand.

Just as Carly and Nellie were finishing up, a man knocked on the diner door. Nellie went to the door to tell the man politely that they were closed and what had happened.

The man began speaking without giving Nellie a chance to explain. "Hello. Nellie Garrett?"

"Yes, I'm Nellie."

"Ms. Garrett, I'm Anthony Page. I'm the attorney for Mr. Ed Madry. Folks told me that I might find you here."

"Won't you come in, Mr. Page," Nellie said. "This is my good friend, Carly Jansen," Nellie raised her hand toward Carly.

Mr. Page acknowledged Carly. "Nice to meet you, Carly." Looking back at Nellie, he said, "Could we sit for a few minutes? I have some papers for you to sign."

Nellie couldn't imagine what this was about. Mr. Page sat at a table; Carly busied herself behind the counter. Before sitting, Nellie asked, "Can I get you some coffee, Mr. Page?"

"No, thank you." He opened a folder and continued. "I'm sure you are aware of the fact that Mr. Madry had no living relatives, no close next of kin, anyway."

"Yes, since his wife died, he's been pretty much on his own." Mr. Page continued, "Mr. Madry came to me many months ago to update his Will and I have here a copy of that Will for you. He has left you the diner and, I might add, debt-free. He was aware that you were the one that has kept it running so efficiently all these years and he was also aware that this was your only source of income, other than social security, of course."

Nellie sat back in the booth; her mouth opened. She had no words. Tears filled her eyes. How life can take such unexpected turns, she thought. All Nellie could manage to say was, "Well, I never, I mean, well, I never. Oh, my goodness." She took a napkin from the dispenser on the table and wiped her eyes.

Carly came over to the table and put her arm around Nellie's shoulders. "That's wonderful, Nellie."

"Ms. Garrett, I just need you to sign these pages where I have marked stating that you have been given a copy of the Will and you agree with things as they are set forth." He handed Nellie the papers and a pen.

Nellie glanced over the words through watery eyes, past the legal garble, and read the summary details. She nervously took the pen and signed at the designated places. "I never, I just, I mean, I had no earthly idea Ed would do this." She tried to regain her composure. "I thank you, Mr. Page."

He stood and reached out to shake Nellie's hand.

Carly followed him to the door. Nellie didn't stand, her legs felt weak. She said, "You come by again when I'm open for business and I'll fix you the best food you've ever tasted."

"I'll do just that, Ms. Garrett. You take care and good luck." Carly closed the door and turned toward the table. "Oh Nellie, that's wonderful, just wonderful."

"Oh my, I don't know where to begin, what to do first."

"Why nothing," Carly said. "You just come to work and do like you've always done. There will be some bookkeeping and other matters that you will need to learn, but you already know all there is to do—just keep doing everything you've always done."

The two women hugged with excitement.

Nellie started behind the counter and said, "I've got to get things in order so I can be ready to open for customers tomorrow."

Carly's thoughts came back to her own reality. "And I've got to go to the library in Erwin to get started on the research for my assignment."

"What assignment would that be?" Nellie asked.

"Things have been in such a turmoil; I haven't had time to even tell you, Nellie. Mr. Bennett called me with an assignment for writing a series of articles on the history of the town and surrounding area. Looks like I'm going to be a journalist after all, that is, if I can do a super job with this assignment."

"You'll have no problem," Nellie reassured. "That's what you went to college for, isn't it?"

"Yeah, but this is the real McCoy! I better get going. You're going to be alright here?"

"I'm fine, just fine. Think I'll make myself a glass of sweet tea and let it all sink in a while. You go on to the library. And, one thing, I might be able to help you out on some history that you won't find in any book—you know, some human-interest point of views." Nellie laughed.

Chapter Sixteen

In the town of Erwin, Carly parked in the small lot next to the public library. She gathered her notebook, pen, and her list of questions for her research.

When she found the reference section in the library, she heard someone call her name and turned to see Thorne Davenport standing at the other end of the aisle. They walked toward each other.

"Hello again, Carly," Thorne said, just above a whisper. "Imagine running into you here."

"Yes. I'm here doing research for an assignment I have for the newspaper. I'm excited really. You know I went to school to be a journalist, and now my boss has given me this opportunity."

"Very good. What is the subject of your assignment, if you don't mind me asking?" Thorne said.

Carly was a little surprised when Thorne showed interest in her project. Scott had always been so involved with his own work that it was the topic of most of their conversations. "It will be a series of articles on the history of the town and the surrounding area. I'm looking forward to it."

"I've lived around here, in Dunn, a few years but I don't know much about the history. I would, however, like to hear about it from you." Before he gave it much thought, he asked, "Would you like to grab a bite after you finish your research?"

"Sure. I'm just checking out a few books and will do my reading at home. Give me 15 minutes," she said, almost sounding too anxious. Thorne was a rugged type of good-looking man. He seemed strong and sure of himself, but not boastful or full of himself. This was the second time Carly had seen him. She could not control the nervousness she felt when she was near him. *Maybe not nervous, but what? It seems like I lost all normal thinking.*

"I'll wait in the lobby area. Take your time."

Thorne was on his cell phone when Carly entered the lobby, so she stood near the door waiting for him. *I wonder how old he is,* she thought. *I like his voice. Oh my, I feel like a schoolgirl.*

"Ready?" Thorne interrupted her thoughts. "How about pizza?" he suggested.

"That will be just fine." One night of eating against her diet couldn't hurt anything, she convinced herself.

During their dinner, they talked briefly about Ed's death and Nellie now owning the diner. Carly asked, "What kind of investigations do you do mostly, Thorne?"

Without going into details, Thorne said, "Quite a variety of cases come our way, mostly through word of mouth. We have handled everything from trusts to missing people."

"It seems like your job would never be boring." Carly immediately thought of *missing people. Maybe he could help her find the diary writer and her children.*

Thorne sipped his beer. "It's not boring, except for the paperwork; that gets a little tedious at times."

"How long have you been an investigator?"

"Gosh, longer than I like to remember, but 20 years, plus or minus. I started law enforcement training after high school but finally changed to investigative work because that's where my interests and, you might say, where my talent lies." His eyes seemed to twinkle when he smiled.

They finished their meal and said their goodbyes. Thorne wondered why Carly had not brought up the subject of the search for her biological mother.

As Carly drove home, all she could think about was Thorne and how she felt when she was with him. She looked forward to seeing him again.

When Carly arrived home, she saw Scott sitting in his car in the driveway. He got out of his car as she walked up the driveway. He kissed her on the cheek and asked as they walked to the front door.

"Where have you been? I thought you were off work most of this week."

Carly didn't exactly like the accusatory tone in his voice but decided to make the conversation about her interests. "Oh, I've got the best news, Scott." She didn't give him time to interrupt her. "Mr. Bennett has given me an assignment, a real assignment. He wants me to write a series of articles about the history of the city and surrounding areas. Isn't that fantastic?"

"Well, yeah, it is," Scott remarked.

"I haven't figured out all the angles yet, but I'm working on it. In fact, that's what I was doing today. I was at the library getting some books for research."

"This late?" Scott sounded more suspicious than before.

"Well, I did run into the investigator working on finding my mom."

"I thought you were going to drop that idea, Carly." Scott followed her into the house. Dinkle met them as they entered the door.

"Why did you think that? I'm not going to drop it. Anyway, it shouldn't matter to you," Carly sarcastically added.

Scott snapped back, "I'm the one who will have to go through the heartbreak with you and all the sorrow you are going to feel when it turns out to be a disaster."

Carly placed the books on the bar in the kitchen. Changing the subject, "That was so bad about Ed at the diner."

"Yeah, poor guy. He wasn't exactly the healthiest person in the world."

"You know, Scott, you are just about the most negative person I've ever known. What's eating you, anyway? Is there something wrong?"

"Wrong? No. You just seem to be so independent these days, like you don't want me to be a part of your life."

Carly filled the coffeepot with water, put the beans in the grinder, and started a fresh pot of coffee brewing. She had been more independent since her parents died and she bought her own house. "You might be right about the independent part."

"And the part about me in your life?" Scott asked, showing his lack of confidence.

"I haven't thought of it like that. Lately, I have felt that you are not that concerned about what affects me. You are very busy with your work, and we hardly ever see each other, except to have dinner on a rare occasion." Carly added, "You know, it seems our relationship is actually more platonic than romantic." She poured their coffee and placed a cup in front of Scott at the bar.

Scott immediately pushed his cup aside. "You know, I can see the writing on the wall. I better go. You think about it Carly and when you decide, you let me know, OK?"

Carly didn't know what to say. This was something she had never expected from Scott. Before realizing it, she was saying, she blurted out, "Have you found someone else?"

Scott didn't answer. He walked out the door, and out of Carly's life.

She looked at her watch. *It's too late to call Nellie. What was that all about? My goodness? Have I been blind and naïve?* Dinkle came up to Carly. She reached down and picked her up. Tears came to her eyes. She said aloud, "You know, Dinkle, life is such a mystery. You never know what's around the corner. But I am so glad I have you, my little furry buddy."

She kissed Dinkle on the head, took her to the kennel, and gave her a bedtime treat. She would take a shower tomorrow. Right now, all she wanted to do was go to sleep of the week working on her assignment.

Surprisingly, she had a little sadness about Scott not being in her life. She had never had a relationship break off so abruptly, but then again, she had never had a long relationship with the guys in her life. Everything would work out, she assured herself. Carly stopped by the diner nearly every day to have lunch. Nellie was getting along very well. She had hired a bookkeeper, so she was free to do her routine jobs of cook, receptionist, waitress, and checkout clerk. She was right, the diner was her home, and the people were her family.

When Carly was having lunch at the diner on Thursday, Thorne came through the door. They had talked on the phone a few times about the steady progress he was making in finding her real mom. Carly motioned for him to come over and join her.

"Hey, Thorne. What brings you by?" Carly's smile showed her happiness to see him. "Join me, if you like."

"Thanks, I will." Thorne put his briefcase beside his chair and took a seat across from Carly.

Nellie, the waitress, appeared. "Well, Mr. Davenport, it's good to see you again. What can I get ya'll today?" Nellie didn't have an order pad; she could remember the orders without writing them down. They gave Nellie their order.

Carly looked at Thorne and asked, "Have you found out anything yet?"

"Well, that's why I'm here." He looked at Carly. "I was on my way to your house Carly, but I saw your car in the parking lot, so I stopped in." Thorne cleared his throat.

Carly didn't realize she was holding her breath, her muscles tight with tension. *Oh no,* she thought, *I don't think I want to hear this. Can I go through with it?* A million questions and thoughts raced through her mind. She spoke hesitantly, "Did you find her?"

Customers came in the door of the diner. Nellie realized that she was standing there, listening. She broke in, "I'll get your lunch and be right back. I guess I'll have to hear about it all later." She looked at Carly. "It'll be alright, honey."

Thorne cleared his throat and began sounding more personal than business. "Yes, Carly. I have located your mom, she is alive. She is married and lives outside Atlanta, Georgia." He stopped talking. Carly's face was pale, with no expression except for the watering of her eyes. Thorne reached for her hand. "Carly, I know this is a lot to take it. Remember, one step at a time. There is no rush."

Nellie noticed the interaction between Carly and Thorne. She brought the sweet tea to their table and refreshed their glasses. She saw the tears in Carly's eyes. "He found her," Carly said softly. Nellie put her arm around Carly's shoulders. "That's great news, sweetie. It'll be all right. We're here with you." Nellie comforted Carly. "Sorry, sweetie, got to get back to my customers." She saw Thorne's hand reach out and cover Carly's hand.

Thorne slowly let go of Carly's hand. "Would you like for me to drive you home, Carly? We can come back later for your car?"

"No, that's OK. I'll be fine." Carly looked in Thorne's eyes and she saw the tenderness in them. She dabbed her eyes with her napkin. "Thorne, maybe you could follow me, and even stay with me for a little while?"

"Absolutely," he said without any hesitation. He helped her with her chair, stopped by the counter, and told Nellie, "Keep the change, and thanks. I'm going to see that Carly gets home OK."

Nellie thought that man was so right for Carly. She never did belong with Scott. Then aloud, she said to herself, "Things might just work out after all," and waved at Carly as she left the diner.

Chapter Seventeen

They arrived at Carly's house. Thorne opened the car door for her. Without speaking, they walked up the sidewalk. Thorne took her key and unlocked the door. Dinkle, as usual, was the happy greeter. Carly reached down and picked up Dinkle.

"Hey, girl. I'm home. Have you missed me?" She gave Dinkle a hug and went to the kitchen to fix his Filet Mignon.

Thorne followed them and said, "How about I fix you some tea?" He put the kettle on the stove.

"That would be nice," she said, placing Dinkle's food bowl on the floor. She freshened his water and sat down on a barstool. She felt anxious and numb at the same time. While the tea was steeping, neither Carly nor Thorne said anything. Thorne could only imagine how Carly was feeling.

Thorne took the cups from the cabinet and poured the tea. "Let's have it on the patio, want to?"

Carly followed him outside. She looked at Thorne and asked, "What now? What do I do next?"

Thorne pulled his chair a little closer to Carly, cleared his throat, and said, "It's up to you Carly. There's no rush, no rush at all. Your mother doesn't know that we have located her. I have her home phone number. When you are ready, you might give her a call. Or, alternatively, you could write her a letter. And, of course, there is also the choice of not contacting her at all."

Carly sat quietly, thinking of her choices. She could not choose to do nothing, but could she take the chance that her mother didn't want her? "You know, I've come this far without her. I've had wonderful parents, who will always be my real parents in my mind. If it turns out bad, at least I have that to remember."

Thorne, surprised at the confident way she spoke, said, "You just let me know what I can do. I have the folder of information in my car."

They sat quietly together. It was a clear, sunny afternoon with a slight breeze. Dinkle scratched on the patio door. Thorne got up and let Dinkle outside, where he made sure all the smells were the same, and then lay down near Carly's feet.

Thorne had another thought. "We could go to Atlanta."

Carly immediately spoke up. "Oh no, I couldn't do that for sure. I think I will contact her by phone."

"When you get ready to call her, will you call me? I would like to be here if you want."

"I would like that," said Carly. They sat quietly for a while.

Carly interrupted the silence. "I have to finish my article series for the newspaper. I don't have much more to write. It's been interesting, I have learned a lot, but it's still not what I want to do with my writing. I want to write novels."

Thorne heard the phone ring. "You want me to get that?"

Carly nodded. He went inside, answered, "Hello, Carly Jansen's residence."

"Oh, Thorne, is that you?" Nellie asked. "Yes, Nellie."

"How's Carly? Is she alright?"

"As expected, a little shaken, but she's going to be fine. We're having some tea out on the patio, just talking."

"Oh good, I'm so glad you are with her. I was just checking. I better get back to work. Ya'll take care, give her my love."

"Thanks, Nellie. I will."

Carly and Dinkle came back inside. "That was Nellie, just checking on us. She sends her love."

"Would you like more tea, Thorne?"

"No, I'm fine. I'll run out to the car and get that information for you."

He returned and gave the folder to Carly. She did not open it but turned and walked down the hallway to her office. She placed it on her desk. *Not just yet, maybe tomorrow*, she thought. She went back to the living room.

"Carly, if you're alright, I guess I'll be going. It's been a rough day for you, so just relax and try to get some rest."

"I think I will. A hot bath sounds good, and then early to bed."

Thorne walked closer to her. "Carly, I hope you know I care about you and that you can call me anytime." He wanted to say more but decided that this was not the time.

Tears came to her eyes. She leaned against Thorne's chest. He hesitated but then put his arms around her and held her close. She looked up at him. Carly wanted to be in his strong arms forever. She wondered if his caring for her was personal or just the way he did business. *No, it was personal. She knew it.*

Dinkle broke the moment, barking a couple of times. Carly looked down at him. "Are you jealous, Dinkle?"

Thorne laughed. "I better be going." He looked at Dinkle, "You best get over it, Dinkle. I'm bigger than you." He kissed Carly on the forehead. "You call me anytime. I'll be here."

"I will, Thorne. Thanks so much, more than you know." After Thorne left, Carly and Dinkle took a nap on the sofa.

Chapter Eighteen

Carly spent Friday morning proofreading her articles and making minor changes. After printing the final version, she went to the newspaper office to give them to Mr. Bennett. She knocked on the office door.

"Come in," Mr. Bennett said, seeing that it was Carly. "Well Carly, how are you?"

"I'm fine, Mr. Bennett. I hope you are."

"Oh, can't complain." He offered Carly a chair in front of his desk. "Sit, please."

Carly handed him the folder. "Here are my articles on the history of the city and surrounding area. It was rather interesting. I tried to include several areas of interest, geography, population, business, culture, special events, and human-interest stories. Anyway, I hope you approve. And, of course, if there are any changes you would like made, let me know."

"I'm sure it will be fine, Carly. I have a meeting in about 30 minutes, so I will review your work later today." He put the folder on the pile of other papers and folders on his desk. "How's life been for you since you moved to your house?"

"I truly love the house. Life is good. I go by the Green Hornet and have lunch with Nellie just about every day and she's doing good."

"I know, it was so sad about Ed. He wasn't that old, but I do believe his health was rather poor."

"Yes, it was a real shock for Nellie. But everything worked out for her in a good way. You know that Ed left her the diner."

"Yes. Yes, I heard about that. Well, Carly, I need to get ready for my meeting. I'll be in touch."

They shook hands. "Thanks again, Mr. Bennett."

Chapter Nineteen

It was early afternoon when Carly got back home. The sky was overcast. Rain was predicted. A good time to read more of the journals, she thought. She retrieved the two boxes from her office, took them to the living room, and settled on the sofa. She took out the journal from 1981 and began reading.

February 19, 1981, 1:10 p.m. Thursday, at work.

I don't have anything to do at work so I thought I would sound busy and type out my thoughts.

You know, I look back over my 31 years and I try to see myself objectively. I see so many things I should have done differently. Last night at the Chinese restaurant, Allen's fortune cookie said, "As we advance in life, we learn our abilities." My fortune said, "The life you lead should be your own."

I have never led my own life and I have never known my potential. I really think now for the first time I'm thinking about the future. I have had some very, very low times in my life but when I met Allen, I think I was at my lowest. Everything has a reason, I believe.

For our first year or so we did nothing but party, drink, have fun, and think of no tomorrow or future of any kind. Allen, not me, went swimming in an outdoor pool in the thunderstorm. Allen showed me another kind of life I had never even known existed.

All through that time I never forgot my children, I tried to cover the pain by partying, but it somehow seeped through. The truth is, I hurt every minute from not having them and cried myself to sleep most nights.

Allen and I got married on May 31, 1980

I used to play the piano for release, but I don't have one and if I did, I wouldn't be able to play it like I like or what I wanted to.

My day will come for everything in my life to be right, I just know it will. My kids will understand and love me, my finances will be completely straight, I'll have a piano, I most of all will be satisfied with myself totally. I honestly hope all these things can happen, but I know I will never love again, and I will never get married again. I will also never have to do anything out of need or necessity of survival, other than of course the normal, eat, sleep, etc. I feel better already just typing this paper. I'll probably be seeing you a lot more. Me.

6-25-81

Allen sat on the coffee table; I was on the couch. "It is over, Allen; it will never be any different."

He pulled a .22 pistol from his pocket—BANG, black spot on his shirt, ringing in my ears—

Oh, my God. You did it—you shot yourself—on my God!

"911."

"Please, this is a real emergency." My mind knew to state clearly the name, address, and problem.

Open the door— "Please help me! I don't know what to do. Hang on Allen! Hang on! Don't you die! Don't you die! Don't you go away!"

The cop leaned down to me. "Ms. You can take your hand off his chest, we'll take care of him. What is your name and relationship to this man? Was there anyone else in the apartment when this happened? Could you tell me what happened?"

Carly felt like she was reading a mystery novel that you couldn't put down. The man shot himself, oh how awful. She spoke aloud, "I have got to find out where this woman is."

It's strange that she never signs her name or mentions who she is, she thought. She doesn't even write her name in her journals.

Carly took a break and went outside. The idea came to her that maybe the neighbor down the street knows something. The pie plate she had brought was clean and, since it was not suppertime yet, she slipped on her sandals and walked down the street to Donna Brewer's house.

When Carly rang the doorbell, the man came to the door. "Can I help you?" he asked.

"Hello, you are Mr. Brewer?"

"Yes. What can I do for you?"

"I'm Carly, Carly Jansen. I live in the next house down. Your wife was so nice to bring me a pie a couple of weeks ago to welcome me; I wanted to return her pie plate." Carly couldn't help but notice the man was short, chubby, and bald with a belly that hung over his belt. "Come on in, Carly. Donna is in the den. By the way, you can call me Charlie. Everybody else does."

"Thanks, Charlie."

He called to his wife as they entered the hallway to the den. "Honey, Carly's here, from down the street."

"Hello, Donna," Carly said when she entered the den.

"Well, my goodness, what a pleasant surprise. Oh, honey, just put that plate on the table there. You didn't have to bring it back, I've got plenty." Donna gestured toward the chair beside the sofa. "Have a seat, Carly."

"I can't stay but a minute."

"Nonsense," Donna said, adjusting the sofa pillows behind her back. "How are things? Are you getting settled in your new home?"

"More and more every day. I have a few little boxes left to sort through. It feels like home."

Charlie stopped by the doorway and announced, "I'm going to ride up to Bob's. I'll be back in a bit." He was out the door before any response could be made.

Carly was startled and she jumped at the sound of the motorcycle starting. "Oh my, I didn't mean to jump."

Donna shrugged, "Oh yes, Charlie—everyone calls him Harley, Charlie."

73

Carly smiled. "Donna, I'd like to ask you a question."

"Anything," Donna's interest perked.

"Did you know the people who lived in my house before I moved in?"

"To tell you the truth, not well. In fact, not at all really. First, the guy moved in, his name was Josh. It wasn't long before a lady moved in with him. Never found out what relation they were, maybe friends, or brother and sister, maybe husband and wife. Just not sure. Anyway, I took them a cake, you know, like I did you, just wanting to be neighborly and all. Josh came to the door and thanked me for the cake, he was pleasant enough, but I could tell right off that he didn't want anyone snooping in his business. Not that it seemed he had anything to hide, nothing like that, just stand-offish."

Donna changed her position on the couch. "Oh my, I hadn't even thought about offering you something to drink or eat."

Carly quickly answered, "Oh no, I just had lunch not long before I came down. I really need to be getting back soon." She didn't want to seem too pressing on the subject, but continued, "So you never got to know the woman?"

"I never met her. All I know is that soon after that bad wreck, I believe in 1994 it was, she must have moved away. I never saw her after that. Don't really know what might have happened. She probably had a very difficult time accepting the fact that a pregnant woman died in that accident and living around here with the memories." Donna looked at Carly. "Why do you ask?"

"No real reason," Carly fibbed. She stood to leave but sat back down. "Do you remember her name?"

"No, don't recall ever hearing it."

Carly added, "I can only imagine how horrible it would be to have been an accident where someone died." She got up again. "I really do need to get back home. Dinkle will wonder if I've abandoned her."

Donna stood. "I understand, but I do hope you will come back. We don't get much company way out here in the country."

"I'll do my best. You're welcome to visit me as well. Again, thanks so much for the pie, Donna. Tell Charlie, Harley Charlie, I said it was nice meeting him."

Donna stood at the doorway as Carly walked down the porch steps. "Don't be a stranger Carly. I'm here most of the time when I'm not at church or out visiting folks."

On her walk back home, she wondered why no one had known the woman who lived with Josh. Surely, she did something besides staying at home. Somebody had to know about them. Maybe she could talk to Thorne about it, but she didn't want to share the journals with anyone just yet.

"Hey, Dinkle, I'm home," Carly said as she entered the house.

Chapter Twenty

After she finished her breakfast Saturday morning, Carly washed the few dishes left from the night before, made her bed, and dressed in comfortable sweats. She wanted to spend most of the day reading the journals. She and Dinkle settled in their usual places to begin the journals from 1982.

1-1-82
Happy New Year. Had a great time. Got to bed at 7:00 a.m., slept till 2:00. This year has to be better than '81. Allen shot himself, Bruce got me for non-support, I quit my job, got arrested in Georgia. WOW, terrible year! Have good vibes for '82.

Carly stopped reading. What had she missed? The journals from 1981 did not mention the surgeries, the court issue for non-support, or the arrest in Georgia. She was sure she would have remembered those stories. She read the entry again and then continued.

1-2-82
Slept late. Since I found out I have hypoglycemia, my waist has gone from 29" to 24" but I haven't lost any weight. It's great. Allen goes to the hospital tomorrow. He is scared. I'm going to take my needle punch and crossword puzzles and a book while I sit and wait. He keeps saying how rich I'll be if he doesn't make it through the operation. I know everything's going to be fine. Melanie called me tonight. They had a nice Christmas. Now that my visitations are regular, things are better.

1-3-82
Allen is at the hospital. I did two needlepoint butterflies while there. I came home so I could get some rest for tomorrow. I went by Mom and Dad's on the way home.
I'm going to sleep with MeMe, my teddy bear, tonight.

I love my diary. I plan to keep one every year so I can leave my life to my kids. I love them so much. I've learned not to dwell on all the things I'm missing, and I cope with it better. Goodnight kids, I love you.

1-9-82

Called to tell Bruce I was picking up M&J at 10:00 (to abide by the rules). He gave me some lip, but I got them anyway. I took them to Mom and Dad's. Got Melanie a perm. It turned out pretty good. Jeremy and I went to the grocery store. Got them a lot of goodies.

P.M. Jeremy went to the movies. Melanie went dancing with her friends. I am worried about her. I have a good relationship with my kids, which means a lot to me. I wish their daddy would drop dead. I tucked them in and slept well.

1-11-82

M&J called. I wish they didn't have to live with Bruce. My neck has been hurting for over a week. I guess it's tension. Goodnight kids. I love you all. God keep you safe. Someday I'll give you peace and happiness, I promise.

Mom

Carly turned the journal over and laid it on her lap. She put her feet up on the coffee table and rested her head on the back of the sofa. She wondered about her mom, her birth mother. Had she kept journals all these years? Did she whisper goodnights and I love you to me at the end of her days like this woman did? Did she even think about me?

Maybe she had children when she got married and those children took up all her time and thoughts. Maybe she had forgotten all about me. Tears flowed, wetting Carly's hairline. Carly let the tears flow with her feelings of sadness. Would she ever get to really know her mother? Her thoughts then turned back to the journals. I must find out who this woman is, who the children are, and where they are. Surely, they would cherish these writings. Maybe they are estranged from their mother and wonder about the same things I do, she realized.

She raised her head, reached to the end table for a tissue, and wiped her eyes. Dinkle licked her hand. Carly said, "I know girl, I'm OK, just a little sad inside."

1-17-82
The kids called to tell me happy birthday, but they were with their dad, and I could tell they couldn't talk the same.

Carly stopped reading and thought about her own birthdays. This woman was younger or about her age when she was writing these journal entries. What a life this woman had led. How sheltered I have been, thought Carly. She continued to the next entry.

1-27-82
I got a kitty! "Four Roses" call her Rosie.

Sept 2, 1982

Hi kids,
   I thought this afternoon that you may not have my new address. It's in this envelope. I hope you write to me every chance you get. I think it was awful for daddy to make you go to your grandma's instead of coming here. It's like you're in prison, going from one cell to another.
   I know you will be busy and tired the first few days you're there. But I would like to know all the little and big things that you do and feel. How is your house and neighborhood? Are there any people your age near you? When you go to school, I want to hear how it is, your teachers, what your school is like.
   Make sure you get a neighbor's or friend's phone number, so you'll have someone to call if you need to. If you can't get a neighbor, just call the police. Melanie, I hope you don't have to get the whole house in order. It's a big job and you need to concentrate on school. I really hope ya'll come and live with me and Allen. It will be so much better for you.
Love you all the way up to the sky, Mommie (mailed 9/4)

Thoughts for Court 11-20-82

I don't think anyone of importance seems to understand the seriousness of the next court date or this whole situation! It is imperative that S&R come to live here. Before M&J left them, M would give them the love they needed, their bath, emotional support through B&R's fights, etc.

M would call and let S&R talk to me. Bruce is mentally sick, and no one seems to understand. I've seen S&R twice since court. They are full of fear and know only how to stay in their room. S said it wasn't fair for M&J to get to stay and them not. I told her, "Mommie really wants all of you to live with her. Maybe the judge will let you and Renee come too!" S said, 'I'm keeping my fingers crossed, Mommie.'

Saturday morning S&R didn't come out of their room till I went to get them. They're like little prisoners with no feelings to show because of fear. Renee's glasses were filthy when we got her. Her hair was over her eyes. Her eye that have something wrong with it is still bad. B&R hasn't even tried to find out what is wrong. The whole time they are with me, I hear 'I wish we could stay here; I miss you Mommie, I wish we lived next door so I could come here a lot.'

I love them very deeply. Their future emotional and mental well-being is my concern. I want them talking to me when they have a problem, when they are happy, or when they just have something to say. Please see the light and truth, Judge. I want to give my kids a life of trust, love, and honest values, to be themselves, with confidence; I could go on and on.

Carly closed the diary after reading the last entry from 1982. She decided to go to the diner for lunch and see Nellie, just to clear her mind and see some of the people in town.

Chapter Twenty-One

The following Monday, Carly went to the newspaper office regarding her latest assignment. Mr. Bennett called her into his office. "Carly, come in, have a seat."

Carly sat down in the chair in front of Mr. Bennett's desk and, as always, he got to the point immediately. "First of all, I want to tell you that you have really been doing a fine job with the assignments."

"Thank you, Mr. Bennett. I appreciate your giving me the opportunity."

He cleared his throat. "Let me get right to it. Harry, you know he writes our human-interest story every week, events in the community."

"Oh yes, I read all of his columns," Carly said with admiration. "Well, Harry called me this past weekend. He's having somewhat of a family crisis. His parents are both getting on up in years and their health has been failing of late. Harry feels he needs to take some leave from work to take care of them."

"Oh, I'm sorry to hear about that," Carly said.

"Since you have done such an outstanding job thus far, I would like for you to take over writing Harry's weekly column while he's away."

Carly almost choked on the air. She could not believe what she was hearing. Trying to control her excitement, she said, "For real? I mean, yes, I mean I would consider it an honor; in fact, I do consider it an honor that you would even ask me." So much for being calm, she thought.

Mr. Bennett smiled. "I know you will do a fine job. No doubt in my mind. If you run into any snags, let me know. I'll help any way I can." He stood up from his chair and reached out to shake Carly's hand. "Welcome to the world of journalism, Miss Jansen."

Carly stood, grinning from ear to ear, shook Mr. Bennett's hand. "Oh, Mr. Bennett, I don't know how to thank you."

"You are welcome, Carly. Harry has already turned in his column for this week, so we will need yours starting next week."

"OK, I'll get right on it." She turned to leave and said, "Thank you again, very much, Mr. Bennett." She was walking on air with weak knees when she left his office.

Carly went back to her desk, gathered up a few papers before she left. She could not get to the diner fast enough. Her thoughts were racing, considering all the possible subjects she could write about on a weekly basis. Nellie could help her get some ideas, she thought. Only a few people from the lunch crowd remained in the diner when Carly arrived. Nellie took one look at her and saw that she looked like a little kid at Christmas. Carly sat on a stool at the counter. Nellie didn't give her time to speak before she said, "OK, tell me, tell me now. Did Thorne ask you to marry him?"

Carly didn't even let the question register. She just blurted out her news. "Nellie, you are not going to believe this!"

"What? Tell me, what is it?"

"Well, I went to the newspaper this morning to turn in my assignment. And you will never guess."

Nellie's anticipation was turning into frustration. "For heaven's sake, Carly, what is it?"

Carly whispered, "Mr. Bennett asked me to be a journalist, to write an article every week, you know about the community, the human-interest story. Isn't that fantastic?"

"Why yes, it surely is, but not surprising. I guess Mr. Bennett is finally seeing your potential." Nellie got a mug from the counter behind her, placed it in front of Carly. "You want coffee?" she asked as she reached for the coffeepot. "But what about Harry? I thought he was the one that wrote those stories for the newspaper," Nellie asked as she poured the coffee.

"Yes, he is, or he was. His parents are sick, and he is taking a leave to take care of them. Of course, I know that's not good news, but I can't help feeling so excited about doing this." Carly took a sip of coffee. Her expression became more serious. "All I have to do is figure out what I'm going to write about."

"You'll do fine, girl. I'll help you in any way I can. Why, folks around here like to read just about anything, especially when it has to do with other folks in the community."

"I can't wait to tell Thorne about it." Carly finished her coffee and put the money on the table. "I better get going, Nellie. See you later this week."

"OK, honey. You take care," Nellie said.

Chapter Twenty-Two

That night, Thorne called to let Carly know he would be arriving back in town Wednesday afternoon. He was in the Raleigh area working on a missing person case involving a young girl.

Carly asked, "Did you find the missing girl?"

"It's a long story. I'll tell you about it when I see you, but yes, we found her and she's fine."

"I'm glad you are getting to come back early. Am I going to get to see you?"

"That's why I'm calling. Want me to pick up some Chinese on my way?" Thorne asked.

"I'd like that," Carly said.

"OK, I'll see you around dinnertime." They hung up.

Carly knew that her new weekly article would take up much more of her time. She wanted to get through as many of the journals as possible. It was Dinkle's bedtime, so she put her in the kennel. She didn't feel very tired, so decided to start reading the 1983 journal entries. When she opened the book, she noticed that the first entry was not until July. She realized there were never entries around the holidays, not even Christmas. I guess without her kids the woman didn't feel much like celebrating holidays, Carly imagined.

7-16-83

You know it's been a while since I have written. I guess from the time in my life where the previous pages ended till now, there's been one crisis after another, whether big or small, I always go to the extreme.

Last September ('82) Allen and I moved into this house. Melanie and Jeremy have been here since late September. I wish Sara and Renee were here too.

8-1-83

Melanie, Jeremy, and Allen are still sleeping. Allen is recuperating from his kidney stone.

All my life it seems I dive head over hills into any project, lose interest, or the challenge leaves and I quit. I would like to set myself ONE goal and work as long or hard as needed to attain that goal.

I don't have a piano now. One day I will. Two of my kids are here and besides, I guess normal teenage crisis, are perfect. Sara and Renee, I can't really discuss yet, except to say, I'm coping.

September 27, 1983, Thursday 4:45 p.m.
Yesterday was hectic! I'm missing Sara and Renee more and more. I've always missed them. Melanie got a gorgeous suit and shoes last night, today she's getting the ends of her long hair permed. Friday she's going to be Miss Junior for her high school parade. Very proud of her.

October 4, 1983, Tuesday 6:10 a.m.
Melanie looked pretty in the parade Friday. Sara and Renee will be here someday.

October 6, 1983, Thursday 6:00 a.m.
Killer headache! I worked hard but enjoyed yesterday. Last night, Allen was in one of his damnable moods. We can be happy then suddenly, wham! It causes me so much tension. He says the cruelest things.

October 11, 1983, Tuesday 6:00 a.m.
Like always, storms blow over.

The journal ended. Just before the holidays, Carly thought. If the woman had written every day, it could be made into a novel. I wish I knew the details about her life. She writes her feelings, but how did she grow up? What kind of childhood did she have? Why do her children not live with her? How did she get two to live with her and not all four of them?

Carly had so many questions. She looked in the box and there were three more little books, one from 1984, 1985, and 1986. She took those three and put them on the coffee table. Wondering if there were possibly more boxes in the attic, she went to the hallway and Dinkle watched as she ascended into the sky once again and barked which meant that Dinkle would wait for her, Carly interpreted. She pulled the string to turn on the attic light.

While in the attic, she moved a few of her boxes around to arrange them more orderly. She looked behind some of the posts and the far corners but saw nothing that had been left by someone else. She pulled the light string, and Dinkle barked as she climbed back down the stairs.

Chapter Twenty-Three

Carly took a shower, dressed in her tan slacks and navy button-up blouse, and brown leather sandals. Dinkle ran to the door, barking before the doorbell rang. Carly fluffed her hair as she walked hurriedly to the door. Thorne stepped inside and, without speaking, he hugged Carly. It felt as if she had not seen him in a very long time. Dinkle broke the mood with her jealous bark.

Thorne slowly released his arms from around Carly and looked down at Dinkle. "OK girl, I know, don't worry, you are still number one." Thorne closed the door. When he turned around, he put his hands on Carly's shoulders, looked into her eyes, and said, "I sure have missed you." He wanted to kiss her. Dinkle barked again.

Carly paid no attention to Dinkle. She said, "I've missed you too, Thorne. Talking on the phone is not quite the same."

"Instead of stopping to get Chinese, what do think about going to the steak house instead?" he asked.

"Perfect," Carly said as she walked to the bar in the kitchen to get her purse. Thorne opened the car door for her. As they backed out of the driveway, Carly said, "I'm glad you found that missing girl."

Thorne said, "Me too. You know, one thing I always find interesting about my work is the different attitudes people have in different situations, especially when they are under extreme stress. In fact, it would make a rather interesting book." He reached over and put his hand on Carly's arm. "Oh, my mistake, you're the novelist, right?"

Carly laughed, "Almost."

They arrived at the restaurant and were seated at a table in the corner. They placed their order and Thorne said, "Tell me what you have been getting yourself into while I've been away."

Carly wanted to tell him about the journals, but instead told him about her new temporary assignment as a journalist, her weekly column, and some of the ideas she was considering. She said, "You know, I might just make it to becoming a journalist after all. Then, who knows, maybe even a real novelist."

"I never doubted it for a minute," Thorne said.

"You know, Thorne, in all the time we've spent together, you haven't told me very much about your life. Where did you grow up, any siblings, you know, all the important facts a journalist needs to know? For starters, how old are you?" Carly said, smiling as she looked into his eyes.

Thorne smiled but then took on a serious expression and started, "Once upon a time, there was a little boy."

"Oh Thorne, you know what I mean." Carly wiped her mouth with her napkin.

"You said you wanted a story, madam reporter," Thorne said.

Carly said, "OK, OK. Now go ahead, tell me the story."

He continued, "For starters, I'll be 44 on November 8." He glanced down at the table. "I don't see you taking notes." Carly just looked at him but said nothing. "I'm a Scorpio, if you believe in that kind of thing." He waited for Carly to inject a thought, but she sat quietly.

"OK, let me see now. I was born in Charleston, South Carolina, and spent most of my childhood there. My family moved to Richmond, Virginia, when I was in my teens. After graduating from high school, I attended the University of Virginia in Charlottesville. Academia is not my forte, I guess you could say. Besides, when I was a boy, a cop is all I wanted to be, you know, the usual little boy dreams, fireman, policeman, or cowboy." He smiled and saw that Carly was listening intently. "What about you? What did you dream of becoming?"

"Unlike the other girls I knew who wanted to be a nurse or schoolteacher, I wanted to write stories and become a famous author." She paused, then said, "Go on with your story first, Thorne."

"Well, I finally decided to enter the field of law enforcement and enrolled in the Northern Virginia Criminal Justice Training Academy in Arlington. At least that's where it was back then. It has since moved to Ashburn. After graduating, I joined the police force in Richmond."

"Why did you quit the force and become a detective?" Carly asked.

"I guess a simple answer to that would be that I got tired of putting my life in danger for nothing."

"For nothing," Carly questioned.

"Yep," he said. "We would chase down and capture the bad guys, then some hotshot lawyer would tell the judge something from a law book and the bad guy is back out on the street. I guess you could say it is job security, but it became very frustrating."

"I can understand why you felt that way. It seems that so many of the bad things that happen are caused by people who have been arrested a few times and set free."

They finished their meal, and Thorne motioned to the waitress for the check.

On the drive home, Carly took up the conversation. "So, you became a detective in Virginia?"

"Yes, in Richmond. After I first started working as a detective, I had to come to Dunn to checkout some information on a case my firm was investigating. That's when I met Sandy. She was the secretary at a lawyer's office where I had to meet with a client."

"Sandy?" Carly asked.

"Yeah," said Thorne. "When I met the client at her office, Sandy was very helpful in typing the papers, witnessing forms, setting up my appointments, all the things that secretaries do. After a week or so, we had lunch a few times, then dinner, and became quite good friends, in fact."

"You traveled from Richmond to Dunn a lot?" Carly asked. "No, the company paid for me to stay in a motel. The investigation took a couple of months."

"Did you and Sandy keep in touch after you went back to Richmond?"

"Yeah, we would call each other and talk about what was going on in our day-to-day lives. I drove down a couple of times on the weekend to be with her. We had quite a bit in common, it seemed. As time passed, we became closer and when the opportunity came for me to transfer to Dunn, I took it. The agency in Dunn needed an investigator because one of the guys was moving away. So, I ended up in Dunn."

They arrived at Carly's house. "Can you come in for a while? I have to know the rest of the story and I have some tomatoes and cucumbers from the garden to give you."

"Sure," Thorne said. "How about the hot peppers, got any of those?"

Carly laughed. "Tons, and you can have them all. I don't see how you can eat those things."

"I guess I have a gut made of steel," Thorne said.

Carly looked at him as they entered the house and added, "But a heart of pure gold."

Thorne shut the door and asked, "Where's the ferocious, jealous guard dog?"

"I put her in the kennel before we left, since it was close to her bedtime, anyway."

"So, the coast is clear?" Thorne asked but didn't wait for an answer. He took Carly in his arms, kissed her briefly and gently on the lips. He looked into her eyes, "My heart of gold is just for you, my dear, just for you." He could feel his heartbeat quicken. He had not intended to kiss her. It just felt natural.

Carly felt the tenderness in his embrace. She could have melted into his arms.

As they walked into the living room, Carly said, "That was a delicious meal. It was nice to have dinner somewhere besides the grill."

Thorne patted his stomach. "Good food and I'm stuffed."

Carly walked over to the sofa and motioned for Thorne to sit beside her. "OK, now where were we? You had moved to Dunn. Then what happened?"

Thorne thought and continued. "Let's see. It was the early 1990s. I rented an apartment in Lillington, worked most of the time and, as you might guess, I saw Sandy more often as time passed. After about a year of dating, I asked her to marry me. She was 22 and I would soon be turning 24. We were married, she moved out of her apartment into mine. That was in late 1993. We were looking to buy a home later."

Thorne abruptly quit talking and cleared his throat. Carly sat quietly and waited, sensing Thorne was having a little difficulty talking about this.

He cleared his throat again. "We found a house we really liked. Sandy had just found out she was pregnant, and we wanted to settle in a home before the baby came." He paused and in a lower voice said, "We were very happy and had a lot to look forward to with the baby and the house and all. But it all came to a halt, a sudden horrible complete stop."

Carly put her hand gently on his arm. "You don't have to tell me all this, Thorne."

He said, "No, you need to know about it. Sandy's car was in the shop, so we only had my jeep. She had a doctor's appointment that morning and I needed to be in Lillington until lunch. So, we drove to Lillington, she dropped me off at the little café down the street from the courthouse and she drove back to Dunn to her doctor's office." He paused.

Tears filled his eyes. "She never made it. There was a wreck. She was almost eight months pregnant. She didn't have on her seatbelt because it hurt her stomach." He lifted both hands over his face, leaned his elbows on his knees. Calmly, he said in a low voice, "She was killed, and so was our baby."

Carly put her hand on his back and laid her head on his shoulder. "I'm so sorry. How horrible. Oh Thorne, I'm so sorry that happened."

Thorne regained his composure, sat up, and looked at Carly. "It was the worst thing that could ever happen. That was 20 years ago and, of course, I'm so much better now. But it took a while. In fact, this is the first time I've talked about it. I appreciate you listening. Besides, you needed to know."

After moments of silence, Thorne looked at his watch. "I guess I had better get going, it's late," he said as he stood.

Carly stood also. "I really enjoyed our dinner, Thorne." Then she remembered, "Oh yeah, almost forget, the veggies." She got the bag from the kitchen and placed it on the bar. "I picked them last weekend. You know the garden will need to be picked again this weekend. You want to come and help?" she asked.

Thorne walked to the bar and picked up the veggies, "Of course, I want to help but this weekend I need to go back to Raleigh to tie up a few loose ends on the paperwork regarding the location of the missing girl."

"Well, I guess I have to do all the garden labor myself." She tried to sound pitiful.

Thorne continued, "I'll be back in town sometime on Sunday afternoon. I'll come over then if that's OK and we can pick it together."

"I look forward to it and I will definitely save the garden picking until then." She smiled. She could see the sadness in his face. She walked with him to the door. He leaned over and kissed her on the forehead. She embraced him gently, trying to help soothe his sadness. He slowly put his arms around her, gently for a long moment. He whispered, "I'll see you Sunday, OK?"

She said, "I don't think that little kiss on the forehead will hold me until Sunday," and reached up, put her arms around his neck, and kissed him, long and tenderly. "Better," she said. "Much better."

She waved to him as he backed out of the driveway.

As she was getting ready for bed, she thought about Thorne losing his wife and their baby, the woman's life written in the diaries; her life had been full of only good things, nothing bad or traumatic, except of course for her parents' dying.

Chapter Twenty-Four

Carly had completed her weekly column and on her drive home from the newspaper office, she heard the weather report. Rain was predicted for Saturday and possibly Sunday. She decided to stop by the diner to check on Nellie and found her cleaning up from the lunch crowd.

"Come in, Carly. How in the world have you been? It's been a while."

"I know Nellie. I've been busier than usual, with writing the article and taking care of the garden."

"And," Nellie waited. After Carly didn't speak, she finished her question. "Thorne? Have you two been spending more time together?"

"You sure know how to get right to the point, don't you?"

"When it's necessary and speaking of necessary, what can I get you to drink?" Nellie asked.

"Just some decaf if you have it," Carly replied.

Nellie poured the coffee. Carly said, "I just dropped by to say hey and see how you've been. And the answer to your question is yes, Thorne and I have been seeing each other quite a bit, at least when he's not out of town."

"I didn't realize he traveled so much in his work," Nellie said. "He doesn't usually, only when a case comes up that requires him to be away. He has been in Raleigh working on a case about a missing girl."

"Oh my, that's terrible," Nellie said caringly. "What happened?"

"Thorne said they found her, and she was fine but as usual, he didn't give me details. He needs to go back to Raleigh this weekend to tie up loose ends and do some reports. He will be back home Sunday, though."

"Are you sure I can't get you something to eat, Carly?"

Carly decided she didn't want to fix supper that night and said, "On second thought, I think I'll have one of those Cobb salads you make Nellie, with the dressing on the side. To go, of course."

"Coming right up," said Nellie. When she returned with the food and handed the bag to Carly, she said, "Got any plans for the weekend?"

"Not really. I was going to pick the garden and work on my flowers, but I heard on the weather report that they are predicting rain on both days. So, maybe I'll read and just relax, or even work on next week's column." She paid Nellie for the food, and then added, "I was thinking, Nellie, it's time I looked at the folder Thorne gave me, you know, the information about my real mother. I've been avoiding the subject, but it isn't going to go away. I may as well find out how things are going to turn out so I can get on with my life."

Nellie said, "I'm sure that has not been an easy decision, but it sounds like you have it under control, sweetie. You know I'm here if you need me."

"I know, Nellie. I'll be all right." Carly took her salad and turned to leave.

Nellie said, "Oh yeah, I meant to tell you that I have enjoyed your articles. You put a real human touch to them, you know, with feeling."

"Thank you, Nellie, I appreciate your telling me that. It's always nice to hear a compliment." Carly smiled.

"See you next week," Nellie said as Carly left the diner.

When Carly arrived home, Dinkle was happy to see her as always. She went to her bedroom and changed into a comfortable sweat. She said to Dinkle, "It's just you and me this weekend, Dink. I'm going to read to you, would you like that?" Dinkle jumped up as if to say, "Come on, let's get started, but feed me first."

In the kitchen, she gave Dinkle fresh water and opened a can of her favorite Filet Mignon dog food. Since she was going to spend quite some time reading, she made a teapot full of tea, rather than just one cup.

She poured the dressing on her Cobb salad and took her supper to the coffee table in front of the sofa. While she ate, she turned the television to the local news. Rain was still predicted for the weekend as well as cooler temperatures. Perfect weekend, she thought, to relax and catch up on the journals.

She finished her salad and took her plate back to the kitchen, poured a second cup of tea, and returned to the sofa, Dinkle settled in next to her. The journal from 1983 had ended in October. She picked up the 1984 journal from the coffee table and flipped a few pages to see perhaps if this one had any entries for the holidays. There were only two pages filled with writing, beginning in May, the rest of the book was blank. Carly scanned another journal. The entries were like the others, missing and loving her children.

The words in the journal were beginning to run together. Carly yawned and then put the journal on the coffee table. Instead of putting Dinkle in her kennel and going to bed, she laid on the sofa, pulled the knitted Afghan over her.

Maybe tomorrow she would open the folder about her birth mother, she thought. Dinkle on her feet, they slept through the night.

Chapter Twenty-Five

When Carly woke up Saturday morning, she stayed on the sofa for a while, looking out the patio doors. The clouds were gray and heavy in the sky. Rain would be falling soon. Dinkle must have known it was going to rain because she headed to her doggie door to go outside earlier than usual and returned quickly. Carly rubbed her gently. "You are my smart girl. Yes, you are." Dinkle gave her wet kisses on the cheek.

Carly showered and dressed in a floor-length, short-sleeved, soft cotton pink dress that she wore just around the house sometimes. She knew she would not be going anywhere and wanted to be comfortable. She slipped on a pair of cotton socks, no shoes today, she thought.

She left her room, and as she passed her office, she looked at the desk. The folder was there. She stared at it for a moment. Should I call today, she wondered. She walked over to pick up the folder, but decided, not today, maybe tomorrow. She was rather certain Thorne wanted to be with her, or at least she wanted him there when she called.

Carly felt hungrier than usual so for breakfast she prepared two boiled eggs, two pieces of buttered wheat toast, sliced tomato, and a glass of orange juice. Dinkle had her usual. She put the dishes in the sink, the coffee was ready, and so she poured a cup just as the phone rang. She looked at her watch and wondered who would be calling so early.

"Hello."

"I hope I didn't wake you."

"Hey, Thorne." She smiled automatically at the sound of his voice. "No, you didn't wake me. I've already had breakfast. Are you still in Raleigh?" Carly asked as she leaned on the barstool.

"Afraid so. I just wanted to see how you are this wonderful bright sunny day," he said.

"Oh, funny you. It is very cloudy; rain all day, they say. Is it raining in Raleigh?"

"Mainly cloudy, just a few light sprinkles," he said, taking a sip of his coffee. "So, what are you planning to do with yourself today?"

"First of all, I was going to pull a few weeds from my flower garden. But with the rain, I'm not sure what I'll end up doing though. I may make some notes about ideas I have to write for my column. I may even break down and watch some television."

"Well, I wish I was there with you now. The other reason I'm calling is to let you know that I'll be home earlier tomorrow than planned, probably by lunchtime."

"Great! Will I get to see you, or did you forget about your promise to help me pick the veggies?" she said jokingly.

He laughed. "I thought I would come by your house on my way home and, no, I haven't forgotten my promise to pick the garden."

"Wonderful."

"OK, see you then. Have a good rainy day," Thorne said.

Carly picked up her coffee mug and went to the sofa. She thought about Thorne coming over. Maybe she would read the information about her mom while Thorne was with her. He had not pushed the issue about her biological parents. She figured he was just thoughtful that way and was leaving it up to her.

"Well Dink, are you ready to hear some more of the story?" Dinkle said yes with a tiny bark. Carly opened the journal from 1985, flipped through the pages to see if it was as short as the previous one had been. Again, she saw that it ended in November, still no holidays.

1985 journal:

July 16, 1985, exactly 35-1/2 years old.

Life is a trip for sure. Tonight, I believe Allen and I are finally ended. An era or way of life has ceased to be. My mind has been in utter chaos for about two weeks, probably all my life but we'll just talk about the present. I don't know what I'm feeling. I must take some time to get in touch with myself for real.

Millie wants me to put words to my song "Light Shade of Blue." I don't know if I can or if I want to. The song is pure with feelings. Words would tarnish it somehow.

Mom came through her surgery. I heard my dad tell my mom he loved her for the first time in my whole life.

God, please keep helping me. I want Jeremy to feel proud of himself and honest and good. I want Melanie to never settle for less and be able to see and make decisions. I want all of this and more for Sara and Renee. Most of all I hope they know that no mother or anyone has ever loved more than I love them. I've been confused, selfish, wrong, stupid, ill, everything, I'm sure. But I do care more than anyone can imagine.

I loved many ways in my life, some good, not-so-good, or bad. Love you can't describe—you feel. True love is unselfish. Not to the point of being made a fool of. You need self-preservation to take hold at times. I love my kids more than anything. I'm learning to love my own self.

July 17, 1985, 10:15 p.m.

Boy! When I learn to make decisions, I go all out! I gave my two-week resignation at work. They say too much major stress is not good. I need a little time to just be and think and sort out things. I've got to look for a job. I hope I find a really good one. I just said everything happens for a reason, I guess I'll see. I guess my next decision is which job I'm going to take—we'll see. Life is one long voyage.

July 28, 1985, Sunday 4:00

In my diary, I can say anything. My thoughts run wild I tell you. I went to see a neurologist Thursday and found out according to him I have a disease or rather a psychotic disorder called manic-depressive. It is mostly hereditary and believe me all the things he described are too true. My neuro-exam was fine.

He sent me to the hospital to have some blood work. I am to take lithium 3x a day, later maybe more and maybe less. It is to get my juices flowing smoothly. It is a mood swing illness, way up and way down—for no apparent reason or no set time. It can be very damaging to someone's life, and I said—believe me! I wrote my brother an 11-page letter Thursday night. I just talked and talked. I hope he takes all of it good. I got a letter from him on Friday.

It was so wonderful. I read it many times. Although I'm pretty sure he doesn't really want me to be his roommate, it was like he felt close to me, the only blood relative that truly loves and accepts him. You know maybe that's another love definition—acceptance. Earlier I said unselfishness. I might learn what it is after all. Even though there are many kinds of love, I'm talking about MY definition.

I don't think no one understands me and I guess that's understandable. I hope this medicine levels me off. I think I'll go soak in the tub.

August 1, 1985
Began Lithium, 300 mg 3x day.

Carly said out loud, "You know, Dink, this poor woman is so mixed up, and more confused than anyone I've ever known or read about. She has a real problem with love. She falls in and out of love every other day it seems." Dinkle was listening but just kept her eyes closed, only her ears twitched. "I sure want to know how her life is now, that is if she is still alive."

10-1-85

I've been on lithium for two months. For the last two weeks or so I have had tremors, especially in my hands and upper body. They were getting worse and even showed in my voice. I called the doctor and he said cut back to 2 pills a day instead of 3. I have gained about 10 lbs.

10-17-85

I'm tired of not ever seeing Sara and Renee. Bruce always has excuses. The last time I saw them was at Melanie's graduation and they weren't allowed to sit with me. I just saw them outside for a while and took pictures.

I called Bruce right before Labor Day weekend and asked if I could see them one weekend a month. It didn't matter what weekend and no notice was needed. I never heard from him.

Melanie called her daddy on October 8 or 9 and asked if S&R could come up here. He thought so but would call her on Friday and say for sure. Sure enough, the answer was no. Melanie was very upset and decided she would go down there. So, after she got off work on Sat a.m. she went there. Things were the same as they were when she went two other times. Sheets were peed on and fleas in the bed, bathtub was covered in mildew. S&R only baths 2 times a week.

Today I went to see a lawyer about custody of S&R. She was very helpful to me.

4:12 p.m. called from the office. Sara answered. She was home alone except the Terminix man was there. It scares me so bad that she and Renee are at home alone, especially with strangers in the house and with the many children who are stolen or molested these days. She was watching Scooby Doo.

She said she had to clean the house and kitchen and make up the bed and study. We agreed to not tell daddy that I called because he would get mad at her.

9:35 p.m. called from 493-6053—Bruce answered.

I said: "Do you think the kids can come this weekend?"

Bruce: "Hold on a second" (asked Ruby) "That's tomorrow, right? Meet halfway? Flimsy excuses. He's got to be somewhere."

I asked him "When then?" He said he needed his desk calendar. I said it doesn't take that long. He said 3 hours round trip. After I asked him again, he said, "How about the first weekend in November?" I said fine. I'll see him at 7:30 on Friday 11-11. Then he started saying something might come up with his work and all. I'm to call next weekend to check on his work schedule.

10-24-85

Jeremy is skipping school—wants to drop out—*and* must take action.

10-26-85

Jeremy wrecked his blue bug—not his fault—the guy ran a stop sign.

10-27-85

Enrolled Jeremy in a different high school, hope things are better.

11:25 a.m. re: visit next weekend—Ruby said that Bruce wasn't there but was planning on calling me today. She didn't know what it was to be. So, I'll wait for his call.

7:20 p.m. He never called and so I called back. We'll meet at 7:30 Friday night and on Sunday at 4:00 at I-95 rest stop.

11-1-85, 3:45 I called Sara—home alone. Bruce told her this morning they were coming; she was so happy and Rene' was too. I am very happy and anxious. Having feelings are so difficult for me to handle.

2:30 p.m. I was at the rest area to pick up S&R. Bruce was about 20 minutes late. The girls and I sang songs and talked all the way home. I did treat them extra special because I hadn't had them in so long. We went to Hardee's and Toys R Us and to Granny's. They spent Saturday night with Melanie. Sun morning was hard just knowing they had to leave. On the way back to the rest area, Sara didn't want to sing because time would go too fast.

Overall, they are doing OK. They go to Sunday School, and they like it. Renee smelled like pee when she got here according to Jeremy. Their hair was oily and not clean. Their panties looked like they had not been changed in several days.

Granny and Granddaddy got them a set of clothes and a pair of shoes, which they needed.

I feel so empty when they go.

Nov 24 '85, 11:50 p.m.

Well, what do you know! Here I am again. I'm beginning to believe in myself less and less every day. The little biddy hope that I may get all right keeps me from just ending it all. I'm tired. I just read all the diaries I've started. Boy, you talk about screwed up. That's me. I can get better and then I slip and fall and get like this and I hide from the world, and nobody knows the agony I go through. I really think I could lose my mind when I get like this. Next thing you know I feel all on top of everything. I'm just tired of it all.

Carly sat forward and placed the journal on the coffee table. She feared that the woman must have committed suicide by now unless things had dramatically changed in her life somehow. Carly wondered if her own mother had ever wanted to know how her life had been. Maybe she had spent many years wanting to talk with her, like the mother in the journals. She could not put it off any longer. She walked down the hall to her office and over to her desk.

Chapter Twenty-Six

At her desk, Carly looked at the folder; the one Thorne had given her, the one that she had tried to put out of her mind. She slowly picked up the folder and walked back to the kitchen where she sat on one of the bar stools with the folder in front of her.

The folder was a plain tan Manila office folder, nothing significant about it. Shouldn't it be gold or purple, she thought, with bold embossed lettering saying *THE PAST AND FUTURE LIFE OF CARLY JANSEN,* or shouldn't the folder be made of fine velvet or silk? She placed her hand on the folder as if the information would seep through to her mind and she wouldn't have to read the words.

Finally, holding her breath, she gently and slowly opened the folder. The first sheet of paper was the agreement that she had signed with Thorne's agency that stated the usual legalize. She turned that paper over. Next was a copy of her adoption birth certificate that she had given to Thorne in the beginning. Her eyes blurred as she saw the next page, this is the moment, she thought. She began to read:

Date of birth: April 28, 1980
Place of Birth: Greenville, North Carolina Weight: 6 lbs. 4 oz.
Given name: Carly Elizabeth Simmons
Carly paused and then continued reading slowly, as if in a daze.
Mother's name: Kathleen Diane Simmons Father's name: unknown.

The certificate was signed by an R.N. and the doctor. It was stamped with the seal of Pitt County Memorial Hospital.

Carly closed her eyes, but the tears still came. She reached for the box of tissues, wiped her eyes, and blew her nose. She read the page again aloud, in a monotone whisper. "Carly—Elizabeth—Simmons—April 28—1980—Greenville—North Carolina—6 pounds—4 ounces—Kathleen—Diane—Simmons—" She repeated the words, "Kathleen Diane Simmons." She just sat still, feelings, no feelings, numb, with disbelief at what she was reading. She felt as if she were dreaming, or like she was someone else.

After a few minutes, she turned to the next page in the folder, which contained biographical information about Kathleen Simmons Richardson. She was married to Tim Richardson. They lived in Georgia, the address and phone number were listed, and Kathleen was self-employed. There was no mention of children. Carly gently closed the folder.

She sat there, unmoving, with no feeling, no thoughts. Finally, she rose from the bar stool, walked over to the sink, filled the kettle with water, and placed it on the stove. She walked back over to the bar, picked up the folder and took it back to her office, and placed it on the desk.

Dinkle was quietly following Carly and watching her every move. After she fixed her tea, she went outside and just stood on her patio. She felt like she was living in a world of fantasy, totally unreal.

Why had the box of journals been left for her to find? Why at this time in her life had she received information about her birth mother? Dinkle let out a couple of tiny barks as if to say, snap out of it, I'm down here, where are you? Carly looked down and sat on the porch step beside Dinkle. She began rubbing Dinkle gently. She cried softly. "I'm so scared Dink," she quietly said to her faithful companion. Dinkle licked her hand in understanding.

Chapter Twenty-Seven

Carly slept later than usual on Sunday morning. She let Dinkle out of her kennel. They did their usual morning rituals. She wasn't very hungry so for breakfast she had a slice of buttered toast and a glass of orange juice. Through the patio doors, she watched the birds on the feeders in her backyard. Carly was excited about seeing Thorne today. She wanted to tell him about the journals, but something kept her from sharing them with anyone. They felt private somehow as if they had some hidden meaning just for her.

To help pass the time until Thorne arrived, Carly and Dinkle spent the morning reading the last journal.

1986 journal:

4-11-86
Happy Birthday, Jeremy—I love you.

In the journal, there was a folded piece of lavender-colored paper. Carly unfolded it to see a poem, centered on the page and nicely printed in large print.

To my four children:
I love you very much
I think of you each day.
I hope life is how you want it so, work at it that way.
Take life as an adventure though struggles come your way.
Live it to the fullest each and every day.
Love is hard to find, and sometimes hard to feel, but unconditionally always
My love for you is real.
The older you become
The more you'll realize
That each person deals with things differently inside.
Expectations of others result in disappointment. Don't judge or blame wrongly just let the others choose.
Believe in yourself and be real
That way you can't lose.

I love you and I must say I'm sorry for the mess so far that life has dealt your way.

I look to the future and hope you do too.

Cause one day my sweeties, our dream will come true.

I Love You

All the way up to the sky.

12/25/86 (printed and framed for their gifts)

This last journal had been written almost 30 years ago. Carly wondered if the children received this heart-felt poem as gifts. She took the journals to her office and put them away in her closet. She convinced herself there were many more journals and that this box had just been overlooked when the movers had loaded the things in the attic. Carly had to realize that she may never find out any more information about the woman who had written these journals. She felt like these journals would haunt her forever if she didn't find out who they belonged to and, if possible, the rest of the story.

Maybe Thorne could help her.

Carly felt like she needed to get out of the house for a while. So, when Thorne arrived, they decided to take a drive to Dunn and have lunch and visit a few of the antique shops afterward.

During the drive back home, Carly said, "You know, seeing all those items from the old days sometimes gives me a sad feeling. Does it affect you that way?"

"Sometimes," Thorne answered. "There are some interesting trinkets. Over time, things have really changed in so many areas."

Carly added, "That's for sure. Makes you wonder what this world will be like fifty years from now."

They rode the rest of the way in comfortable quietness, enjoying being together. As they were getting close to the diner, Thorne asked, "Would you like to stop in and see Nellie, maybe grab a bite?"

Carly thought and said, "I don't believe so. I'm a little tired." They rode in silence for a while, and then Carly said, "Thorne, it's time. I'm going to call her."

Thorne was temporarily at a loss for words. This had come out of nowhere, it seemed. He asked, "Your mom?"

"Yes. Yesterday, I finally looked at the information you brought me, and I think that I need to just do it. Rather than keep putting it off, just do it and then I will know the outcome." Carly didn't tell him about the journal mother and how that had helped convince her to talk to her own biological mother. Carly added, "You know, she just may have been wondering about me all these years."

"That's certainly possible," Thorne added.

Chapter Twenty-Eight

Carly and Thorne arrived and as always, they were happily welcomed by Dinkle. She said, "Have a seat, Thorne. I need to feed Dinkle and get her settled for the night."

After putting Dinkle in her kennel for the night, Carly retrieved the folder from her desk and returned to the living room. She placed the folder on the bar. Thorne could sense her hesitation. "Carly, are you sure you are ready to do this?"

Carly opened the folder. "Yes, I've put it off long enough. It's going to be what it's going to be. I just need to get it done so I can get on with my life." She took the phone and folder to the sofa. "Who knows? I might even have a mother in my life."

Thorne wanted to say something to reassure her, but he was concerned that it may not have the hoped-for happy ending.

"I know. I've been over and over the possible reactions and outcomes and now it's time to stop the guessing and find out how it will be. Although I am nervous, I have a pretty good feeling about the outcome. She may just be very glad to finally hear from me, we'll plan when to meet and I might even have some sisters and brothers to get to know as well."

Carly's hands were trembling slightly as she opened the folder and turned to the page with her real mother's phone number. Her fingers felt numb. Her thoughts were on hold. She dialed the number.

After the third ring, a voice answered, "Hello."

Carly was holding her breath and wondered if Thorne could hear the loud thumping of her heart. Finally, she spoke into the phone. "Hello." She paused briefly. "Could I please speak to Ms. Richardson?" Her palms were sweating.

"This is Kathleen Richardson." The woman's voice sounded sophisticated but pleasant enough.

Thorne placed his hand on her shoulder. Carly cleared her throat and continued. "Hello, Ms. Richardson." She felt her throat tightening, her pulse racing, sweat was forming on her forehead. From somewhere her voice came and said, "My name is Carly, Carly Jansen."

Carly wanted to throw the phone across the room and run out the door and never come back. Get hold of yourself, she thought.

"Carly Jansen," Ms. Richardson questioned. "Do I know you?"

Carly took as deep a breath as possible. She had considered all the possibilities but had forgotten to write herself a script. "Ms. Richardson, I am 34 years old, and my adoptive parents died recently, and I decided to search for my real mother and the agency found you and after thinking about it for quite some time I finally decided to call you." Carly stopped talking and felt paralyzed, waiting for the woman's response. Thorne moved his hand on her shoulder for reassurance.

There was quiet from the other end of the phone. Then the woman continued in a tone that sounded so automated and rehearsed that Carly almost thought it was a recording. Authoritatively, the voice said. "My dear girl, I do not know what you think you are doing but you need to get this nonsense out of your mind. The past needs to stay in the past. It can do absolutely no possible good for anyone to bring up the past. Everyone has a life and I suggest you get on with yours and leave me out of it. You are not to contact me ever again. Have I made myself clear?"

The paralyzed feeling left Carly, she felt like she was melting right there on her sofa. She softly replied, "I guess it has to be." No tears. Where were her tears? she thought. "I'm very sorry I bothered you."

She heard the woman hang up the phone abruptly. Carly's hand, still holding the phone, slowly rested on her lap. She sat on the edge of the sofa.

Thorne reached over and gently took the phone, clicked it off, and placed it on the coffee table. Neither of them said anything. Thorne gently put his arm around Carly, pulled her to him, and leaned back against the sofa. She put her face on his chest, and he wrapped her in the cocoon of his strong arms. He felt her body trembling as the tears turned to soft weeping and then deeply felt emotional crying.

Her crying stopped and Carly leaned up from Thorne's embrace. She patted his shirt. "Oh, I've cried all over your shirt." He didn't say anything but reached over and got the box of tissues. Carly pulled out two and wiped her eyes and blew her nose. "Oh Thorne, I'm so glad you are here with me," and she leaned against him. They sat there silently for quite some time.

Thorne was the first to speak. "Let me get you some water, Carly, OK?"

"How about a vodka tonic, or rum and coke, a martini, scotch neat, or maybe all of the above," she said as she leaned forward. Thorne couldn't tell if she was joking. Carly spoke in her normal voice, "You know, I thought I had it all covered. I guess down deep inside, I didn't really believe that she would not want to have anything to do with me." She realized Thorne was still waiting for her answer to the water question. "Oh, I'm sorry. I made some tea earlier, a glass of that would be nice. No ice, please."

"Coming right up," he said and went to the kitchen. Carly got up and walked over to the bar. Thorne just let her talk; he knew she needed to just express everything that she was feeling. He placed her glass of tea on the bar.

"You know she didn't even ask how I am, how my life has been, what I have become, how my health is, am I married, or if I have any children. She is very bitter sounding, at least toward me. What did I ever do to her? She's just a cold-hearted you-know-what."

Thorne silently filled in the correct words and agreed wholeheartedly. He sat on the bar stool next to Carly and let her continue, allowing her feelings to flow and form into words.

"I guess she really didn't want me from the very beginning. There weren't any extenuating circumstances. I was probably the product of a one-night stand or something worse. She just didn't want to bother with me. Maybe she was a drunk, maybe a prostitute. I'm glad I never knew her. I'm glad she didn't keep me. I'm glad about it all. I'm not sorry for her one bit." She quit talking. The tears began to flow. Thorne took a few steps back to the sofa, picked up the tissue box, and handed it to Carly.

Carly continued, in more of her normal voice. "You know, it's pretty obvious that she has never wondered about me. I'm sure she has never tried to find me." She looked at Thorne. "Well, I guess I know how it ends. Now I can get on with my life."

Thorne put his arm around her shoulder, leaned over, kissed her on the cheek, and whispered, "I'm sorry, Carly, so sorry." Thorne could only imagine how she was feeling, the rejection is so final from the person who gave birth to you. He knew she would have all kinds of mixed emotions as time passed. They returned to the sofa and sat quietly for a long time.

"I'm so glad I had my good parents, my real mom and dad," Carly said, then she fell asleep. Thorne held her.

He thought about his own baby and how precious she would have been, and he truly could never understand how someone could give away their child, no matter what the circumstances. He felt sad for his loss, but Carly's pain was different. This was no accident with a horrible ending but rather an outright decision made by a living person. Thorne gave a brief thought to investigating Ms. Kathleen Richardson just to find out what he could do to shed some light on the reasoning for her actions.

Not long after midnight, Carly woke up, but she didn't sit up. She wanted to feel the comfort of Thorne's arms as she lay on his chest. She slowly sat up, ran her fingers through her hair. "What time is it? She asked, reaching for a tissue."

"It's after midnight."

"I'm sorry about all my ramblings," Thorne spoke. "Totally understandable."

Carly stood. "It was so sweet of you to stay with me. I'll be fine, now, I'm sure." She looked back at Thorne. "It's so late. You are welcome to sleep here on the sofa tonight rather than drive home."

Thorne considered it. He cared so much for her and was concerned that her "*I'm fine*" words may be a front to keep him from worrying. He said, "You've had quite an emotional upheaval. You can't expect to get over this in a few minutes or a few days."

"I know. I'm not sure I will ever really get over it. Right now, I wonder if the pain will last forever." Carly looked at Thorne. "So, the sofa tonight?"

"OK, if you are sure that it's OK."

Carly sat beside him and took his hand in hers. "Thank you so much for being with me and comforting me. It has helped so much. I would not have wanted to be alone through this."

"I'm here for you anytime," Thorne said, and he leaned close and kissed her.

She got up from the sofa. "I'll get you a pillow and a blanket." She got them from the linen closet and brought them to the sofa.

Thorne asked, "Do you think you will be able to get any sleep tonight?"

She answered, "In one way, I feel like I could sleep a very long time, but in another way, my mind doesn't feel like it will rest at all."

Thorne put his arms around her. "Goodnight. You come and get me if you want to talk or anything."

"Thanks, Thorne, I will." She walked down the hall to her room. Lying in her bed, she quietly said to no one, "She doesn't want me. She has never wanted me." No tears, just a blank mind, empty heart, and total numbness is all Carly felt.

Chapter Twenty-Nine

Carly had a restless night. She would awaken with thoughts of the phone conversation or rather the words Kathleen had said to her. The words kept going over and over in her mind. *Absolutely no benefit to anyone. Never contact me again. Get on with your life and leave me out of it. Absolutely no benefit to anyone. Never contact me again.* Then she would think of the poor woman who wrote the journals. She wished her mother had felt that way. Her mother had not ever wanted her and probably never even thought about her.

Carly put on her robe and went to the kitchen. Thorne had already made coffee for himself and had a glass of cranberry/pomegranate juice sitting on the bar for Carly. He looked at Carly. "Guess there is no need to ask how you slept."

She let Dinkle out the doggie door and returned to sit at the bar. "Thank you for the juice. Glad you found the coffee," she said to Thorne. She looked out the patio doors and observing the colorful flowers blooming in her garden, she said, "You know, it takes different things to make a beautiful flower, the stems, the leaves, sometimes thorns, the roots, and the dirt. You could enjoy a rose-filled life and may even get pricked by a thorn along the way. The words I heard from my biological mom were thorns, maybe the only thorns I have ever experienced, to be honest."

She thought about the woman who wrote the diaries—she wasn't crazy or mentally imbalanced; she just lived a life full of thorns and it seems, no blooms.

Thorne interrupted her thoughts. "Will you be calling Nellie today? I'm sure she will want to know how it went with the call."

Carly looked at her watch. "Probably after her breakfast rush. I'll give her a call. Maybe she can come over. I'd like to tell her in person."

Thorne drank the rest of his coffee. "I'd better get going. You're going to be OK?"

"Yes, I'll be fine." She walked to the door with Thorne. "And I know I can call you anytime," she said before he had the chance.

She tidied up the sofa, washed the cup and glass. She was not hungry at all. Then she called Nellie and she agreed to come over after the lunch shift.

Just as she hung up the phone, it rang, startling her briefly. "Hello."

"How is the most wonderful, beautiful, caring person in the world doing?" Thorne said.

"Hey, Thorne," Carly answered. "I'm OK, really. I called Nellie and she's going to come over after she closes the diner this afternoon."

"Oh good, I'm sure she wants to know how things went." Thorne was parking his car at his office. "Well, I'm at the office now. I'll talk to you later today."

For a second, she realized the relief she felt that Scott wasn't here. She knew he would have no sympathy or understanding. I told you so would have been his response, she knew.

Carly was so happy to have Thorne in her life. She needed to work on her column for the newspaper, but just went to her office and sat quietly at her desk. Dinkle followed her and guarded the door. After a short time, she pulled out her notes, jotted down a couple of ideas but found that she was not able to concentrate. So, she went outside and pulled weeds from her flowers. She picked a few of the flowers, put them in a vase, and placed it by her kitchen sink.

Dinkle followed her to the sofa. They both fell asleep.

Carly was awakened by the doorbell and Dinkle's barking. She looked at her watch as she got up and walked to the door and opened it. "My goodness, Nellie, I fell asleep on the sofa. I can't believe I slept this long. Come in, come in. Have a seat, let me just wash my face and try to wake up. Make yourself at home."

Nellie took one look at Carly and knew she had been feeling sadness and stress. "You go ahead, honey. I'll take a load off and rest my tired bones."

Carly returned to the living room. "Have you had a busy day?"

"Oh yeah, there was a convention or something in town and evidently somebody told the folks that the diner was the best place in town. Whew! I haven't seen that many people for breakfast and lunch in a long, long time." Nellie put her pocketbook on the floor beside the chair. "Well, enough about me. What's going on, honey?" Carly sat on the sofa and began. "I called her, I called Kathleen Simmons Richardson." She stopped briefly.

Nellie could see immediately that the outcome had not been good at all. She got up from the chair and joined Carly on the sofa. "Oh honey, what in the world? What did she say?"

Carly said in a matter-of-fact voice, "She simply said that absolutely no good for anyone could come from this and for me to get on with my life and leave her out of it and never contact her again." Nellie put her arm around Carly and the floodgates opened. In between sobs, Carly said, "Oh Nellie, I had it all figured. I knew that anything was possible but when it came right down to it, I never truly believed that it would be this way." She pulled out tissues and let the tears flow.

Nellie said, "Now, now, honey, I'm so sorry. You'll be all right, just go ahead and cry, let all the hurt out. I had no idea it would turn out this way when I suggested that you go ahead with the search for her." Nellie could not understand why in this world a mother could say those things. She wanted to go to Atlanta and give her a piece of her mind and more.

Carly got control and wiped her eyes. "I know Nellie. I just can't explain what I feel. I don't even know what I feel. The extremes of all possible emotions."

"When did you call her?" asked Nellie.

"Last night. Thorne and I went to Dunn and when we got back here, I made the decision to get it done."

Relieved, Nellie said, "So, Thorne was with you when you called?"

"Oh yes, Nellie, he was so wonderful, so kind and calming."

"I'm glad he could be here. I wish you would have called me. I would have been glad to come over and be with you," Nellie said.

"I know, but you have to get up so early in the mornings and I was fine. There is nothing that anyone can do, really. Thorne sat with me for a long time. He was so understanding. I fell asleep, I guess from the exhaustion of emotions and crying. When I woke up, it was after midnight, so I invited him to sleep on the sofa. He was already having coffee when I woke up this morning."

Carly realized she had not offered Nellie anything and said, "Look at me, I'm so caught up in all this, I forgot my manners. Would you like some lemonade, Nellie?"

"No honey, nothing, I'm fine." Nellie looked out on the patio. "Let's go outside and sit in the fresh air. It's not too hot this afternoon. How does that sound?"

Dinkle followed them to the patio. They sat quietly for a while.

Nellie said, "Your flowers are very pretty."

"I enjoy them. It seems the weeds grow more than the flowers, though." Carly reached down and picked up Dinkle. "My little vegetable garden has done pretty good too. It's my first try at a garden and I'm surprised at how many veggies I've picked from it. It seems the more you pick, the more they produce."

Nellie thought back. "Yeah, my husband and I had a garden almost every year. I canned a few tomatoes each year. There's nothing like a home-grown tomato with mayonnaise for a sandwich. I've sure eaten my share of them."

"Thorne and I have them sometimes for lunch. That patch of hot peppers on the edge of the garden is just for Thorne. He eats hot peppers like candy."

Nellie could see Carly's face brighten when she talked about Thorne. "Have you ever had fried green tomatoes?"

"I saw the movie," Carly replied. "But, no, I've never tried them."

"Well, next time you come to the diner around lunchtime I'm going to have to fix them for you. There's nothing quite like a fried green tomato. When my husband was living, I was always afraid we wouldn't have any tomatoes left on the vine long enough to turn red because he sure loved the green ones fried." They sat for a long while, each in their own world of thoughts. Nellie stood up. "If you're sure you're going to be OK, I'll be getting back home."

"Really, I'm fine Nellie, don't worry. I'll definitely call you if I need you." Carly followed Nellie through the house. When Nellie was walking to her car, Carly said, "Next time I come to the diner, if you're not swamped with customers, I'll try some of those fried green tomatoes."

On her drive home, Nellie could only think about calling that woman and telling what a sorry person she was and how much she had hurt Carly. How could a mother say those horrible things to her own flesh and blood? She turned the radio on to a country music station and help get the bad thoughts out of her mind.

Chapter Thirty

Carly closed the door and almost tripped over Dinkle when she hurried to answer the phone. "Sorry girl," she said to Dinkle and picked up the receiver. "Hello."

"Hey Carly, you sound out of breath. Are you OK?" Thorne asked.

"Oh, I'm fine. Nellie just left and I hurried to the phone, hoping it was you."

"Did ya'll have a nice visit?"

"Yes, we did. I told Nellie about the rejection phone call, and she was sad for me. She was sorry for suggesting the search, since it turned out this way. I tried telling her that she was in no way to blame."

"Well, I can understand how she feels. To tell you the truth, I was feeling rather bad because I'm the one who found the information for you," Thorne said.

"Don't you start now," said Carly. "It's nobody's fault, no one is to blame. We all talked about how many ways this could turn out. Things didn't turn out the way I had hoped, but at least it's over."

Thorne asked, "Are you coming into town tomorrow?"

"I haven't quite finished my article; Wednesday is the deadline, so I'll be in town on Wednesday for sure," Carly said without much enthusiasm. "Why do you ask?"

"Just wondering if we could have lunch?" Thorne thought and then said, "I'll change my plans so that I will be there Wednesday instead of tomorrow, and we can meet then."

"OK, about 11:30?" Carly asked. "At the corner hotdog cafe?"

"That sounds good to me. I'll, of course, talk to you between now and then." Thorne's call-waiting beeped. "I got another call, Carly. I'll talk to you later."

When Carly hung up, she heard a strange sound outside. She looked on the sofa, no Dinkle. She ran out to the patio and looked out over the backyard. She saw Dinkle lying on the ground. Carly cried out as she ran,

"Dinkle! Oh, my god! Dinkle!" She got to Dink and saw that she was still breathing but lying very still. There was a bleeding area near the side of her ear and neck. "Oh, my baby, it's OK Poohdinkle. It's OK."

She picked her up gently, walked back inside, got a towel from the hall closet, and wrapped Dinkle in it. With Dinkle in her arms, she grabbed her purse and hurried to her car. She carefully put Dinkle on the passenger seat. Carly had to keep wiping her tears to clear her vision as she drove what seemed like a thousand miles to Doc Skinner's office. Luckily, there was a parking spot very near the front door of the Doc's office. She walked through the front door and called out. "Doc Skinner?"

"I'll be right there," he said from a room down the hall.

Carly didn't wait. She walked quickly down the hall. "Sorry Doc, but this can't wait. Dinkle has been hurt, she's barely breathing, and she's bleeding."

Doc Skinner came to her and guided her to the next room. "Now, now, let's see what we have here." He opened the towel and briefly looked at Dinkle. "It's not as bad as it looks, my dear." He walked to the exam table. "Just put her right here and let me get her fixed up." Doc Skinner gave Dinkle an injection and cleaned the wound.

"She was hardly breathing when I found her!" Carly exclaimed. "I was so scared she was going to die."

"She was just in shock, Carly, scared mostly, I guess. Have you seen any stray dogs around your place?" Doc asked as he rubbed Dinkle.

"No. Dinkle has a doggie door so that she can go outside when she needs to."

"Well, she's going to be just fine, but you might want to keep an eye on her or go outside with her from now on," Doc suggested. He reached into the cabinet and gave Carly a doggie blanket to wrap around Dinkle.

"I'm so glad you were here, Doc Skinner. Thanks so much." Carly walked out of the exam room with Dinkle in her arms. "You'll send me a bill, as usual?"

"I will. You take care now." Doc Skinner returned to his work.

Chapter Thirty-One

Thorne slid out of the booth and stood to meet Carly when she entered the corner café.

"Have you been waiting long?" Carly asked as she sat down in the booth across from Thorne.

"Nope, I just got here," Thorne said. After the waitress took their order, he asked, "How's Dinkle?"

"She's much better. She seems to be healing quickly, although I believe she might be getting a little spoiled and expects me to carry her everywhere or hold her all the time. Before I left, I put her in the kennel. I can't let her outside by herself anymore. I would die if something happened to her."

Their drinks and hotdogs were brought to the table. Thorne doused his hotdog with hot sauce. He had been wondering whether he should mention to Carly the possibility of locating her bio mom's siblings if Carly was ready for it or if she would even be interested. She seemed to be doing well, so Thorne began, "I've been thinking about trying to locate any siblings your bio mom has or other family members that might know who Kate was dating back then." He got no response so continued. "I did find out that Kathleen has one sister and one brother."

"Are they older or younger?" she asked.

"The sister is older; the brother is the youngest. Anyway, I was wondering if you would like for me to pursue it further."

Carly thought for a moment. "I'm not sure what good would come of it but, on the other hand, I doubt it surely couldn't be much worse. Let me think about it."

They finished their lunch and Thorne placed the money on the table and they walked out of the café. As he opened the car door, he said, "OK, you think about it, and we'll discuss it later." He looked at his watch and said, "I need to get to a meeting with a client. I'll see you tonight for supper." He started to walk away but turned and added, "Tell that ferocious guard dog I'm really glad she's OK."

"I will," she said. Although Carly wanted to ask Nellie what she thought about locating relatives of Kathleen's, she wanted to go home and check on Dinkle.

She missed Dinkle's usual greeting when she arrived home. She laid her purse on the bar and went to the kennel. "Hey my girl," Carly said. Dinkle whined a pitiful greeting. Carly took her from the kennel, and they went outside. Dinkle walked slowly to the yard and back and looked up at Carly. Carly interpreted Dinkle's expression to say, 'I'm through, now you can pick me up'.

"I think you are getting a little spoiled, Dink. This time, you need to make it on your own." With a few hesitations, Dinkle followed her back into the house and Carly closed the doggie door.

That evening, after Thorne and Carly had finished dinner, Carly decided to tell him about the box of writings. She said. "Thorne, when I was putting some of my storage boxes in the attic, I came across a box that had been up there quite a long time. Of course, my curiosity got the best of me, so I brought it downstairs and looked inside."

"What did you find?" asked Thorne.

"It was full of journals and diaries, greeting cards, little notes, just lots of personal things like that. Funny thing though, there weren't any names on any of the writings, at least no real names; only daughter, sister, mother, sweetie, things like that."

"I guess you read everything?" Thorne already knew the answer but asked, anyway.

"Yes, I did. A lot of it was about the same situation. This woman evidently was a mother who did not have her children with her. I couldn't tell exactly why or what had happened. It was just of lot of pain in her writings, sadness, and confusion."

Thorne asked, "You think she may have been a writer?"

"No, it was more personal, about her feelings at different times, except for Christmas time. None of the writings were dated during the holidays."

"How long ago were they written?"

"In the late-70s, mid-80s.

"Wow, that was quite a long time ago."

Carly said, "I think the box was accidentally overlooked during the move. I've asked Nellie, the realtor, and even the neighbor down the street, and no one seems to know anything about the woman. They did mention a guy named Josh, but they didn't know anything about the woman, I was wondering Thorne, could you do a little searching and find out who used to live in this house? Maybe where they moved to?"

Thorne thought for a minute. "Seems like that would be no problem. I'll look into it tomorrow, see what I can find."

"Great," Carly said.

Chapter Thirty-Two

Thorne made a few calls the next day and found the names and locations of the people who had previously lived in Carly's house. He called that afternoon to give Carly the news.

Carly asked, "That was fast work, Mr. Detective. Where did they move to?"

"They live in the western part of the state, in the mountains. Bonnie and Josh Hardin. However, there is no phone listed in their name. They probably have cell phones like everybody these days. However, I do have an address. We could take a gamble on them being home if you want to take a day trip to see them."

Carly hesitated. "If you'll drive," she said. "I would be scared to drive in the mountains."

"Of course, I will, but from what I saw on the map, I don't think Miller's Creek is deep in the mountains, more in the outer area or foothills. It's about a three- or four-hour drive from your house, so we leave early one morning."

Carly thought, "I can't leave too early because I have to make sure Dinkle is fed and everything. Maybe around 7:30; would that be good?"

"What day is good for you?" Thorne asked, as he looked at his own calendar.

"Any day really, as long as I get my article written and turned in to Mr. Bennett by next Wednesday."

"We could do it this weekend if you want."

Carly said, "What time do you think we would get back home?"

"I guess it depends on how the visit goes, but I assume it would be before dark."

"Saturday sounds OK to me."

"Alright, I'll pick up some ham biscuits and be there around 7:00."

Oh boy, more healthy food, thought Carly, which she realized what was beginning to enjoy it. "OK, I'll have juice and I'll make some coffee to take with us."

"Sounds good. I'll be working most of the time today and tomorrow, so I'll see you Saturday morning."

Carly didn't want to leave Dinkle for such a long time, especially with her injury. She couldn't leave the doggie door open either. She decided to call Nellie to see if it would be possible for her to come over after the diner closed on Saturday and check on Dinkle.

Nellie answered the phone. After hearing Carly's request answered without hesitation, "Of course, I will. I'll be glad to do that. You'll just need to write down what I need to do about her food and all. I'm so glad she's better. Don't you worry, I'll be with her when she goes outside, and I'll take the broom with me just in case any stray dog wants to bother her."

Carly laughed to herself at the sight of Nellie in the yard with the broom as a weapon. "Wonderful, Nellie, I appreciate it so much. I'll bring the key by the diner Friday sometime." She was glad that Nellie hadn't asked where she was going, but she's not exactly that kind of person.

Chapter Thirty-Three

Early Saturday morning, Thorne arrived with ham biscuits. Carly had made coffee and filled two thermos mugs for the trip. Carly told Thorne that Nellie would be coming over after she closed the diner to take care of Dinkle. They were on the road by 8:00.

"You say it takes a little over three hours to get there?" Carly asked.

"Yeah, we will probably get there about lunchtime. We could find a place to have lunch and get there in the early afternoon." Thorne said.

"I sure hope she is home," Carly said.

Thorne said, "It's a chance we're taking but there is no way to tell."

Thorne turned onto Highway 421 North. "We're looking for Highway 16 North," he said to Carly. "That will take us to Millers Creek. It's on the other side of Winston Salem, not a big town, more of an outskirt of North Wilkesboro."

"You know I have never been to the mountains," Carly stated. "You're kidding!" Thorne said, surprised. "You have missed something, then. It will absolutely take your breath away in the late fall when all the trees are changing colors. Maybe we can arrange a trip this fall so you can see for yourself. It's really too amazing to put into words."

They rode in silence for a long while. Carly thought about the diaries. Many questions ran through her mind. She said aloud, "I wonder if Bonnie wrote the diaries. Do you know how long they lived in the house?"

"They moved to the house around 1985 or 1986. I couldn't get a clear picture of the details other than like you found out, they stayed to themselves mostly."

Thorne drove past an exit to Yadkinville. After another thirty miles, they took an exit in North Wilkesboro for Hwy 16 North, which would take them to Millers Creek. There were already signs up in the town announcing the annual fall apple festival, as well as a car race coming in September. Thorne spotted a restaurant, *Fire Mountain Grill,* and pointed to the sign, "What do you think? Want to try it for lunch?"

"Looks good to me."

Thorne parked and they entered the restaurant. A little past the entrance at a counter, the person behind the counter asked for their order and collected payment. Thorne had never experienced this order of business in all his travels. "Take a seat wherever you like," the person said.

They chose a table next to a window across the restaurant from the noise of the kitchen staff. "I don't think I have ever ordered and paid before being seated in a restaurant," Thorne said.

"Yeah, I thought that was out of the ordinary too." She looked out the window. "I'm very glad that the weather is so nice for our trip today."

It was early afternoon when Thorne and Carly arrived in Millers Creek. They turned into the driveway, a dirt path really, that was surrounded by woods. Although gravel had been put on the driveway, it was still a rough ride.

Carly said, "Wow, and I thought my house was secluded. This is really private, almost scary really."

Just a short distance down the driveway, they came to a single-wide trailer. It didn't exactly look like a place that was lived in. There were no cars at the trailer to suggest anyone was there. There were carvings hanging on the trees, handmade wooden garden planters in the yard, a carport structure that appeared to be full of storage items, and another closed-in building of some sort. Thorne saw that the driveway continued into a curve, and he decided to drive a bit further. When they rounded the curve to the right, the house came into view.

"Oh my," Carly said. "What a gorgeous house. It looks like a ski resort that you would see in the mountains."

Thorne drove up closer to the house. The property was totally natural woods, a wildlife haven. The deck was on the top floor and contained pots of petunias and other flowering plants, hanging baskets, and a table with an umbrella. Around the front side of the house was a cozy-looking covered front porch. Carly noticed chickens roaming in the yard.

Before they got to the house, two dogs greeted them in a rather unfriendly manner. The black and white Australian Shepherd didn't look happy at all. The little Dachshund, although barking boldly, looked happy to see them.

Thorne parked the car, and a woman came out of the house and stood on the covered porch. She was an attractive woman dressed in jeans and a T-shirt. Her long hair, mostly gray with mixes of blond streaks, hung down her back. It appeared that she would have to take a deep breath to be five feet tall. Thorne rolled down his window. "We are looking for Bonnie Simmons," he announced.

The dogs were still barking, but the woman went to the steps, called out and the dogs came to her, and she blocked them on the porch. When she came down the steps and over to the car, she said, "I'm Bonnie Simmons, and you are?"

Thorne motioned to Carly in the passenger seat. "This is Carly Jansen, and I am Thorne Davenport. We would like to talk to you if you have time."

Bonnie said, "What about?"

Carly leaned over the driver's seat and looked out at Bonnie. "Hello, Ms. Hardin."

"Just call me Bonnie."

Thorne said, "Bonnie, we have a box of writings that probably belong to you. Since you do not have a phone listed, we decided to take a chance on you being home so we could deliver it to you."

Carly leaned forward and said, "I bought a house in Flat Branch a few months ago and found a box of journals and other items in the attic. Thorne is a private investigator and he found out where you had moved. Do you know if you left a box in the attic?"

Bonnie thought for a minute. "I could have, it would have been a long time ago though. I left that house in 1994, but Josh stayed there until we found this house." Bonnie flipped her hand as she realized she didn't need to get into the nitty-gritty details. "Let me see the box and I'll be able to tell."

Thorne and Carly got out of the car. He opened the trunk. Bonnie stayed back a distance, knowing she could use the .38 tucked in the waist of her jeans if they pulled a dead body or weapon out of the car. Thorne took the box out. "Here it is," he said to Bonnie.

When Bonnie saw the box, she knew it was hers. "Why yes, that is mine. Oh my, Josh must have overlooked it when he was packing." Realizing they weren't serial killers, she relaxed and said, "Ya'll come on in. Thorne, you can put the box on the table on the porch." They followed her to the covered porch. "I have the dogs blocked on the deck, no worry."

Thorne and Carly followed Bonnie to the porch. Carly said, "It's such a nice day, and so beautiful and quiet here."

Bonnie said, "Have a seat. Let me get another chair from the deck."

Thorne offered, "I'll do that if you want."

Bonnie was already walking toward the deck. "The dogs. I'll get it." Bonnie returned with her chair. "Ya'll have driven quite a while, could I get you something to drink, or have you had lunch?"

Carly answered, "We stopped and had lunch, but a glass of water would be great."

"What about you, Thorne, coffee?"

"That would be fine, black is good."

Bonnie returned with the coffee and water, as well as a cup of coffee for herself. She lit a cigarette.

Carly commented, "What are your dogs' names?"

Bonnie said, "Sadie is the Australian Shepherd and Molly is the Dachshund. I love dogs, they love you no matter what."

Thorne said, "You have a beautiful home."

Carly replied, "Thank you. You would not believe the miracles that have occurred since finding this place. Really, it has truly been miraculous."

They all sat in silence for some time, enjoyed the sounds of nature. Carly felt comfortable. Bonnie seemed very content and real. Carly wanted to ask her about the journals but didn't know exactly how to start. It was none of her business, r e a l l y . Her journalistic curiosity wanted to know more.

Bonnie broke the silence. "Well, tell me a little about yourselves." Thorne and Carly looked at each other. Carly began, "Like we said, Thorne is a private investigator. I met him after contacting him about locating my biological parents. He found my mom. It took me a while to get up the nerve to contact her, but when I did, she—" Carly was surprised at how smoothly and unemotionally she was telling all this and continued. "Well, she flat out refused to have anything to do with me and basically told me to never contact her again."

"Oh my, that must have been very painful for you," Bonnie said. "To say the least," Carly agreed and continued, "Thorne is going to look for her siblings or other relatives to see if anyone may have information about who my biological father might be. He probably didn't even know about me or if he did, I'm sure he has his life now and will not want it interrupted by memories from the past."

Thorne continued telling the story. "That's right. I found that Carly's bio mom's name was Kathleen Simmons Richardson."

Bonnie tried to hide the expression on her face. "Would you excuse me a minute?" She went back inside and down the hall to take time to get her composure. She was puzzled and stunned. *There are probably a few women by that name. Kathleen, Kate. My sister? This cannot be right; it must be a mistake.* She got herself under control and went back to the porch. "Sorry about that." She took her seat and appeared to be in control, but her mind was very unsettled.

Thorne spoke. "We have taken enough of your time. We just wanted to return the journals to you."

Bonnie interrupted. "You're not leaving already, are you? Please stay. I think we may have something to talk about."

Both Carly and Thorne looked puzzled.

Bonnie said, "You said your biological mother's name is Kathleen Simmons Richardson?"

Carly answered, "Yes, she lives near Atlanta, Georgia."

Bonnie cleared her throat. "My sister's name is Kathleen. We have a brother, Richard, who lives in Florida. We call my sister Kate. But I'm afraid you are mistaken about her giving up a child at any time. She is married, with two children, lives in Atlanta, a good Christian family really."

They sat quietly. Bonnie thought about her sister, back to childhood and through the years. She spoke, "In fact, Kate was always considered a good girl; I mean, I felt like the black sheep most of the time." She shook her head, "No, I can't believe this, not Kate, I'm almost positive."

Bonnie got up from her chair. Carly was afraid she was going to ask them to leave but instead she said, "I'll be right back." She went inside. Thorne and Carly didn't talk but it seemed they both knew what each other was thinking—another dead end. Bonnie returned.

Thorne wanted to try to get more information if possible, so he asked, "Bonnie, do you remember any guys who your sister Kate dated in high school or afterwards? It would have been around 1979 or 1980. Carly was born in April 1980."

Bonnie thought for quite some time and said, "You know, Kate was always so good at getting dates, but she never seemed to 'fall in love' with anyone; dated them once or twice, maybe, but no one really comes to mind."

"What did she do after high school?" asked Thorne.

"Well, let's see. She graduated. Then she went to UNC in Greenville. She took courses and got a degree in interior design. In fact, she is currently self-employed as an interior designer in Atlanta."

Carly said, "Greenville is the city where I was born, according to my real birth certificate. Thorne was able to get that for me. Kathleen Simmons was listed as my birth mother, and she is self-employed. So, I don't think it is a mistake."

Bonnie thought and continued, "Trying to think back. Kate was about 13 when I left home, so I didn't know much about her life. My brother, Richard, was around age 4, I believe. I went home occasionally but not much was discussed about her situation." Bonnie was quiet, thinking. She said, "I just thought about something. I do remember that there was a guy. Kate was seeing him the summer after she graduated from high school. It sounded rather casual though, not serious."

She tapped her lips with her finger. "What was his name?" she asked herself out loud. Then it looked like a light came on in Bonnie's mind and she continued. "You know, come to think of it, Kate did not come home at all during her first year of college. We all thought she was independent, doing well on her own."

Bonnie's face flushed. *Could it be? Could Kate have been pregnant? Is Kate this girl's mother?* "Oh my, I can't believe it, I just can't believe it, but it is making more sense now." She drank her coffee and didn't speak for a time.

Thorne and Carly sipped their drinks and didn't speak. They didn't want to interrupt Bonnie's thoughts.

Bonnie blurted out, causing both to jump in their seat. "Joey, yes, Joey was his name. She wrote about him in a letter to me. I didn't take it as a serious relationship, rather, just catching me up on the latest events in her life." She paused again, lit a cigarette, and continued, "Let me see, his last name. What was his last name?" she asked herself. She kept repeating the name Joey trying to connect the last name automatically. Finally, she spoke, "I have her letters. Let me get them and I'm sure the name is in one of them from that year."

Thorne and Carly sat quietly, waiting for Bonnie to return. When she did, she had a letter opened in her hands, scanning, and said, "Here it is. His name was Joey Saunders."

Thorne took out his notepad and wrote the name on it. He asked, "I guess you don't know anything about where he may be located or any other information that may help us locate him?"

"No, never heard anything more about him at all." She added, "I'm older than Kate, I guess you know that; anyway, as I said, I left home when Kate was around 13. I just remembered our parents talking about Kate not coming home for the holidays that year." She stood and asked if Thorne and Bonnie wanted refills, both declined.

Bonnie didn't hesitate. "I'm sure if Kate was dating him, he had to be in high standing, along with his family. I, on the other hand, was the one who seemed to get the losers, but that's neither here nor there, I guess. But no, I don't really know anything about him. Don't know if he went to college, nothing really."

Thorne replied, "Well, the name has been a great help. We appreciate it."

Carly said, "He probably doesn't even know about me, that is, if he is my real dad. Even if he is, or even if he knows about me, I'm sure he has his life and will not want it interrupted by painful memories from his past."

Bonnie said, "I'm really sorry about how Kate treated you, Carly. I'm still at a loss for words over the whole situation. Our parents would have a heart attack to learn that Kate was less than perfect, I'm sure."

Carly thought Bonnie seemed to feel a little resentment toward her sister.

Bonnie said, "So, Carly, you were adopted?"

Carly replied, "Yes. My parents were good people. I truly felt loved by them. My young life was very good. They both passed away not long ago and that's why I guess I was willing to try to locate my birth parents."

Bonnie asked, "Are you married? Any kids? Where do you work?" She lit another cigarette. "I guess I sound like an interrogator, sorry, none of my business."

Carly smiled, "No problem. No, I'm not married, no kids. I studied to be a journalist and work for the local newspaper. What I really want to do is write novels. That's why I moved to the house in Flat Branch. It is quiet and secluded; a good place to work without the noise and interruptions of the town."

Bonnie said, "I love being creative. You know, I didn't even know that art and creativity existed until I met Josh. But that's a whole other story." She turned to Thorne. "What about you, Thorne, married, kids?"

"No and no," he answered, a little too curtly. He didn't like discussing his life, the pain of losing his wife and their unborn child. "Sorry, didn't mean to sound so short, but no, I'm not married and have no kids."

Bonnie sensed that was all he had to say and didn't pursue it. Carly said, "What about you, Bonnie? You mentioned Josh?"

Bonnie smiled, even her eyes brightened. "Yes, Josh and I are married. If you had a few days, I could tell you the whole story." She lit another cigarette. "What a rollercoaster my life has been," she added.

Hesitantly, Carly asked, "I gathered a little from the writings in the box. Sorry, I apologize for reading your journals. I didn't think that I would ever find who they belonged to. They are very personal."

"No problem, honey. It's all part of life, the worst part really. But, like I said, if you have a few days, I could tell you all about it."

Carly asked, "Could I use your restroom?"

"Sure honey, ya'll come on it. See what a beautiful mansion I've been blessed with." Bonnie led them through the front door.

Carly was awed by the inside. "Oh my, cathedral ceilings, real log walls, so much room!"

Bonnie pointed through the doorway. "The bathroom is just to the right." She turned to Thorne. "Have a seat, Thorne. More coffee or anything?"

"No, I'm fine, thanks." He sat on the sofa. Carly returned.

Bonnie said, "Have a seat, Carly. You talk about wanting to write a book. I wish I had had a goal at your age. I guess you could say my goal was surviving every day," she said regretfully, "but I have goals now and that is to enjoy retirement. I retired early, at 62. I couldn't stand that job for another three years, so I took early social security. This year since I'm now 65, my small retirement payments began. Retirement has taken some getting used to, but I think I'm just about to adjust."

"That's great, Bonnie. Some people don't like retirement." Carly wondered what she meant by surviving every day.

"That's probably because all they have in their life is their job. Not me. I have more to do than I could possibly do. I love crafts, art, playing the piano, flowers, cooking, baking sourdough bread, quilting, knitting, crocheting, and fishing—to name a few things. Speaking of which, I'll give you a loaf of fresh sourdough bread. I just baked it yesterday. It is good toasted." Bonnie went to the kitchen and got a wrapped loaf and brought it to Carly. "Here you go. It's already sliced and if you don't eat it after 4-5 days, you might need to put it in the freezer."

"Thanks so much," Carly said. "I'm sure it will be delicious." Bonnie looked at Thorne. "She can share with you, OK?"

"Sounds like a good idea," Thorne replied. "Thanks."

Bonnie returned to her chair. "You know, I had an art gallery at one time, many years ago."

Thorne asked, "What was the name of your gallery?"

"The Painted Turtle. It was located on Main Street, but it was open only a few months."

"What happened?" Thorne asked.

Bonnie was quiet for a long moment. "It was something I don't like to think about, to tell you the truth. Anyway, it's a long story, very complicated. You would have to know the history to make any sense of it all, I guess. But in a nutshell, I had a good life in many ways at that time. Then the wreck happened." She paused and resumed quietly. "The wreck, the changing point in my life, really. It seemed my life has been categorized in two parts, before the wreck, and after the wreck."

Carly said, "Oh my, I'm glad you didn't get injured." She realized as soon as it came out of her mouth that she had no idea about that.

"I suffered a closed head injury."

Carly added, "Oh my, that is serious."

"It was. More than that, it saved my life because afterward I had a terrific headache one day and when the doctors did tests, they found I had aneurysms which led to brain surgery."

"Oh, no!" Carly said. "That's why you closed the gallery, I assume."

"Yes. In fact, it took many years to recover from all of it."

Thorne asked, "When and where did this wreck occur?"

"It was in the spring of 1994." Bonnie lit another cigarette. "The lady in the jeep was killed." Bonnie's eyes welled up with tears.

Thorne grew very pale, his palms sweaty, he felt a rush of warmth over his entire body along with cold chills down his back. Carly suddenly realized what he had just learned. The atmosphere in the room became indescribable. The air was mixed with pain, agony, regret, sadness, sorrow, and anxiety.

Thorne got up, "Excuse me," he said and went outside. Bonnie looked at Carly. "Is he OK?"

Carly thought about what to say, then she spoke softly. "Thorne's pregnant wife was the one driving the jeep."

Bonnie felt her breath leave. What did she do now? Her past has come back. She had gotten to the place where she could enjoy her days without so much pain and regret and fear. Now this. She got up and walked outside. Thorne was standing on the porch. She walked up to him, placed her hand on his arm. "I'm so sorry, so very sorry, Thorne."

Thorne didn't respond. He just continued to lean on the porch rail and stare at the ground.

Carly stayed in the living room. Her emotions were going in all directions. She remembered her conversations with Maggie and with Donna. The woman who had lived in her house had moved away after the accident. She felt confused and lightheaded. All the emotions she had experienced, the many questions she had had since moving to her new house, and finding the box of writings was beginning to feel overwhelming. She walked to the kitchen and filled her glass with water. She regained her composure somewhat. Bonnie came back into the house. "That poor man. I had no idea. I can't believe it, after all this time."

She looked at Carly. "You know, the box of writings is only part of the story. My life has really been a drama as well as traumatic. You said you wanted to write a novel—well, my story may be some interesting reference material."

Carly couldn't believe what she was hearing. Could all this coincidental circumstance be for a purpose, she wondered.

Bonnie continued, "And, you know, it might just help someone." Then with a brief unfunny laugh, "Or they could just send the white coats—*They're coming to take me away, ha-ha.*" She laughed again. "I guess you're too young to remember that song."

Carly said, "I didn't read anything about the gallery or the wreck in your writings."

"No, you wouldn't have, because the journals were long before that."

Carly wanted to ask where her children were now, what happened but didn't want to bring up more bad memories.

As if Bonnie had read her thoughts, she said, "A whole lot happened from the time of the writings until now. Those journals were written during the worst part of my life." After a moment, Bonnie asked, "Would you and Thorne want to stay for supper?"

"Oh, thanks, but we need to be getting back home. My friend is looking after my little dog, and I need to get back to her. It has been so nice meeting you, Bonnie, and thank you so much for your hospitality and the bread."

"No problem. I just hate that Thorne had to be reminded of such a painful time in his life."

"He'll be fine, no worry." Carly picked up the loaf of bread and thanked Bonnie again and walked outside. "Are you ready to go, Thorne?"

He turned toward her. "Sure, if you are."

"Bonnie invited us for supper, but I told her that I had to get back to Dinkle."

Thorne walked to Bonnie and reached to shake her hand. "It was nice meeting you, Bonnie."

"You too Thorne. Listen, ya'll come back again anytime. Oh Carly, let me give you my cell phone number. I'm serious about telling you about my life if you ever want it to use for one of your books."

Carly added Bonnie's number to her contact list. "Sounds super. I'll be in touch."

Bonnie added sincerely, "Carly, I hope you find your biological dad and that it turns out really good for you."

Thorne turned and thanked Bonnie for her information. "You take care, Bonnie." He and Carly got in the car and drove out of the driveway and for a long way in total silence.

Chapter Thirty-Four

They passed Millers Creek Elementary School, Millers Creek Baptist Church, a small store called the *Creek Stop*. The distant view of the majestic mountains was beautiful.

When they entered the small town of Wilber, Thorne broke the silence. "Are you thirsty, Carly?"

"No, I'm fine," she replied.

They drove through Piney Ridge, West Jefferson, then saw a sign 24 miles to Sparta. Carly asked, "Are you OK Thorne?"

Thorne cleared his throat. "It all came back to me. The morning, the phone call, the hospital, all, it all came back." He cleared his throat again. "I'll be OK, I'm sure. It was just a shock. That's all."

Silence ensued. Thorne turned on the radio to the oldies station. *Make the World Go Away,* Eddie Arnold was singing. Carly's thoughts were on the diaries and the unbelievable coincidence of finding the woman who wrote them. John Denver's *Country Road Take Me Home* was playing.

Carly had told Thorne a little about the contents of the diaries but thought this might be a good distraction for him. So, as they drove through West Jefferson, she began. "You know, the coincidences that happen in life make you wonder if everything is already mapped out for a person."

Thorne turned off the radio and said, "Yeah, I'll say. Who would have ever imagined that your biological aunt was the one who wrote the journals?"

Thorne asked, "Again, when were the journals written?"

"They were dated in the late 70s and early 80s."

Thorne considered the dates. "That was quite some time ago. Why would she have stopped writing then, I wonder. You just bought the house this year. That would have been over 20 years ago when she moved away."

"I haven't got all of it figured out just yet," Carly said. "I haven't got all the details, dates, history, etc. But I have her cell phone number and we will be talking more in the coming days."

"I'm really happy for you Carly. It's good you have met someone in your biological family that you can talk to." Thorne didn't mention investigating her biological dad, at least not right now.

Carly continued, "She told me that her life would make a very interesting story and offered to tell it to me if I wanted to use it for the book I want to write."

"Wow. That sounds pretty exciting."

"It just might be," Carly said. "I need to figure out the best way to hear her story. I mean, it would not be possible for me to take off from work and be away from home and, besides, I'm sure she wouldn't want to tell the whole story in one or two sittings."

Thorne said, "Why don't she record it? She could mail you the tapes as she gets them finished."

"What a great idea," Carly exclaimed.

When they arrived at Carly's house, Nellie met them at the door with Dinkle jumping up and down at her side. Carly picked up Dinkle and gave her kisses.

"How was your trip?" asked Nellie.

"The mountains were amazing," Carly said.

Thorne added, "I hope to take Carly back to the mountains in the fall when all the colors are unbelievable."

They said their goodbyes and goodnights.

The next day, Carly called Bonnie and they agreed that telling her story on tape might be the best way to accomplish this. Bonnie said she had a mini-cassette recorder and would buy some tapes and get started on it.

Chapter Thirty-Five

The next week, Carly received the first tape from Bonnie. Thorne was out of town and she was free the rest of the day so she could begin listening to Bonnie's story.

Dinkle greeted her as always and followed her around while she gathered her recorder, notebook, pen, and then they both settled on the sofa. Carly put the tape in the machine, set it on the coffee table and her phone rang.

"Hello."

"Hey, my beautiful lady," Thorne said.

"Hey Thorne, what are you up to?"

"Same ole, same ole," he said. "What have you been doing?"

She hesitated but then said, "I got the first tape from Bonnie today."

"Oh yeah? Have you had a chance to listen to any of it?"

"I was going to after I finished a little weeding in my garden."

"Oh, sorry I interrupted." He changed the subject. "How's Dinkle doing?"

"She's great, like she was never hurt."

"I'm glad. Listen, I just wanted to check in and tell you I miss you. I'm not sure what time I'll be back. Later today, probably."

"I'll miss you too, Thorne. Call me tomorrow?"

"I sure will."

Carly hung up the phone. After she finished her morning chores, she took Dinkle outside for a while. There weren't too many weeds in the garden after all, and she was proud of how she had kept her garden looking nice. The phone was ringing again as she went back inside.

"Hello."

"Carly, hey, this is Bonnie."

"Oh, hey, Bonnie, perfect timing. I just came inside; I was pulling a few weeds out of my little bed."

"If you're busy, you can call me back."

"No, no, it's fine. I got your tape."

"Good, that's why I'm calling. I wanted to make sure it arrived. Have you had a chance to listen to any of it?"

Carly said, "It just arrived yesterday. I plan to start listening today."

"OK then. I'll let you go. Say hello to Thorne for me."

"I will," Carly said. She was startled when the phone rang again as soon as she hung up. *This is Grand Central today*, she thought to herself.

"Hello."

"Carly, what are you doing today?"

"Hey, Nellie. Nothing really. I just came in from checking on my garden. Why, do you need something?"

"No, I thought I would ride out to sit a bit if that's alright. It will be a little later this afternoon."

"Super. Thorne is out of town, and I would like the company."

"OK, see you after I close the diner."

Carly got her notebook and pen from her desk and came back to the living room, settled on the couch with Dinkle snuggled at her side. She could at least get started on the tape. She pressed the play button on the recorder.

"Hey, Carly." Bonnie cleared her throat. Carly could hear her lighting a cigarette. She continued, "I have turned on the recorder several times and my mind seems to go blank. Anyway, I don't really know where to start. Also, I've been thinking about it all, how to begin, what to include. Then I decided that you could decide if anything was worth keeping or not. So, I guess, here goes. Oh, and keep in mind that I'm not an English major.

"I was born in a small town, Erwin, NC, at Good Hope Hospital, which has since been torn down. My parents lived with my paternal grandparents in Buis Creek. They were farmers, in fact, both of my parents grew up on the farm. My mom's parents lived in Lillington. Mom was from a large family, with 12 or so siblings, but my dad had only two brothers.

"There were three sons and then three grandsons were born before I was born. They thought I was something special and I felt it from them. Nannie just seemed to love me no matter what. She taught me to crochet. Her house was welcoming, with no fancy decorations, lots of dust on the furniture and she fed stray dogs in the house. She was just fun to be with. I always felt so special.

"Let me just add here that my ideas and opinions have varied, changed with age and with experiences. The thoughts I had at age 15, then 25, then 35, then 50, and now at 65, have all evolved and differ or at least are thought of differently.

"My parents were raised on a farm after the depression. When I was born, we lived in a small house down the path from my Nannie and Papa's house. When I was one or two years old, we moved to the city since my dad got a job in Durham. My mom was adamant about leaving the farm, it seems. But we visited both grandparents every other weekend for the rest of their years. Equal time with each was one of the big conversations or arguments between my mom and dad on the trips there and back.

"Most of my growing-up years, I would consider normal, I had everything I needed. I was taken care of, had doctor and dentist visits, did very good in school, but mostly we went to church. We were like Baptists in our beliefs. Every Sunday morning and night, Wednesday night prayer meetings, all missionary conventions, and oh yeah, the AYF—that's the Alliance Youth Fellowship—We were always there unless we were sick or something.

"During my youth, we would always have a few people from church visit. We would sing around the piano as I played after I became good enough at it. My sister sang, as well as my mom. Sometimes on the weekend, we could have friends over for a cookout, hamburgers, hotdogs, and, best of all, hand-churned homemade ice-cream, peach, banana, or vanilla.

"My favorite holiday was Christmas. My sister and I got one nice gift and some smaller items from Santa, oranges, apples, and nuts were in my stocking.

"I had a couple of traumas when I was growing up. I can't remember my exact age. Once when playing on a swing set at a neighbor's house, two doors down from our house. The boy was shaking the swing set, standing on the A-frame part. It came apart and hit the top of my head. I walk fast down the road to home, my head bleeding a lot. My parents took me to the ER, where they shaved the top of my head and put in lots of stitches. In fact, it has been family joke about why I'm not normal. The other time, I closed the car door on my thumb and had to have it stitched.

"I had piano lessons and played the piano in church sometimes. I also accompanied my sister when she sang solos. I played the clarinet in the band in high school. Our band director expected us to practice at home and when he asked us about it, everyone said that they had. Well, I told the truth and said, "No." He suspended me from the band for the next game. I still felt proud of myself for telling the truth.

"My mother was very strict. My dad worked most of the time. I didn't like getting punished. It seemed so unfair because many times, I had not done anything wrong.

"Things changed when I was around 14 or 15.

"Carly, I think I'll take a break for a while. I'll talk more later," Bonnie said.

Carly listened a few seconds more, but the tape was blank. She clicked off the recorder. So far, not much, she thought. *It seemed to be a normal childhood. I wonder how she got to the point of the diaries. I guess I thought she had grown up in a horrible situation.*

Knowing it was about time for Nellie to arrive, she put away the tape player and started preparing lunch; spinach salad with oil and vinegar dressing, whole wheat crackers with garlic butter, and freshly squeezed lemonade.

Nellie was right on time. After they enjoyed their lunch, Carly joined Dinkle on the sofa and Nellie sat in her usual chair near the patio doors.

Carly began, "You know, it seems hotter this year than usual."

"I agree. It's just unbearable, the heat plus the humidity," Nellie said.

"Is everything going good at the diner?" Carly asked.

"Yes, it is. Mostly good days, some a little slow lately. Not having Ed tend to the diner while I run an errand or take a day off has taken some getting used to. Otherwise, it's pretty much the same as ever."

"How are things going with Thorne? I see that the two of you are still seeing each other, even though his job is over."

"Well yes, and no. Yes, we are still seeing each other, quite often in fact. And no, his job may not be over." Carly thought it was time to tell Nellie about the box and the discoveries she and Thorne had made. She said, "Nellie, I need to fill you in on what has been happening."

Nellie said, "I hope it is good."

"Maybe good, but for sure, it is interesting." Carly began. "When I moved here and was putting away some of my things in the attic, I found a box. It was old, very dusty, and had probably been there for many years."

"Was it full of money?" Nellie laughed.

"Maybe something better than that. Anyway, I didn't say anything because it didn't matter, it seemed. I asked around about the people who lived here before me and not much was known. A couple of people said that a guy named

Josh lived here but they didn't know much about the woman that lived with him."

Nellie said, "Yes, I remember when you asked me about that. Did the box tell you anything?"

"No, not the people's name. It was full of letters, journals, and some items that seemed to be memorabilia. I couldn't resist and, besides, I assumed the person who had left it wouldn't return for it. So, I read the journals and letters. The woman who wrote in the journals was very depressed. It seems she had four children and she did not have them with her. All she wrote about was how much she loved them and missed them. I wonder if she is still alive or what became of her."

Nellie said, "There's got to be a way to find out who she is."

"Let me continue. I asked Thorne to try to find out who had lived here previously, and he did. He got the address, but there wasn't a phone listed in their name. So, that's why we took the day trip to the mountains."

Nellie was quiet, wondering what happened.

Carly continued. "The woman, her name is Bonnie, was very nice. She invited us in, made us feel welcome. When Thorne showed her the box, she knew it was hers. I apologized for reading the entries, but she said that was fine. I had so many questions but figured I had pried into her personal life too much already.

"Anyway, the subject came up in my search for my birth mother. When I said her name, Bonnie got this look on her face that seemed like she knew her. She left the room for a moment and when she returned, she said that Kathleen Simmons was her sister, but she could not believe that her sister would ever give a child up for adoption. Anyway, after more discussion, we knew it was true. When Thorne asked Bonnie if she knew the name of the guy her sister was seeing back then, Bonnie came up with a letter her sister had written to her because she had mentioned a guy in it."

Nellie exclaimed, "My goodness, what a coincidence! This is all sounding like a fairy tale."

"I know, right? Anyway, Thorne is going to investigate and see if he can find him. His name is Joey Saunders. He and Kathleen went to high school together, but that's all we know."

"I'm sure Thorne can find out everything you need to know. Let's just hope it has a better ending than the situation with your birth mother."

"Yeah, that's what Thorne is worried about. But I think I can handle it. He may not have even known about me. We'll see."

Nellie said, "Well, I certainly hope it turns out good. You've had quite a bit of excitement these past few weeks; getting to write articles for the newspaper, hopefully finding your birth dad, and meeting your biological aunt."

Carly said, "And that's not all. When I told Bonnie about my desire to be a novelist, she said I was welcome to use her life as a reference."

"What about her life could be a story?" Nellie asked. "Evidently, she has had many rough spots, ups and downs. We didn't get into any details, but she is recording her story on mini cassettes and sending them to me."

"It ought to be interesting. That would be wonderful if it works out that you can write a book about it."

"We'll see. I'll try to keep you updated on what's happening with everything."

"I would like that. You know I'm interested in you." As usual, Nellie got to the point. "I think Thorne has more interest around here than the job."

Carly felt her cheeks redden but didn't respond. "I guess your face tells it all." Nellie smiled.

Carly said, "One problem is that he's quite a bit older than me. He also has been married before and I doubt he is interested in marrying again. I'm pretty sure he doesn't want children."

"Do you want children, Carly?"

Carly rubbed Dinkle and finally said, "It seems I have been just living day to day. Lately, I have come to realize that I haven't thought about what I want other than my desire to be a journalist and to write a novel."

Nellie said, "What would you write a book about?"

"I've been giving it some thought lately now that I have settled into a day-to-day routine. One thing we were taught in college is that when we create stories, we shouldn't tell anyone about it because it will interfere with the flow."

"Well, shucks." Nellie laughed. "I wanted to know all about it as you went along, you know, sort of give you some pointers and ideas."

"I'm hoping Bonnie's tapes will help." She added, "How about your life, Nellie?"

Nellie laughed and stood up. "Let's see, I was born, I was raised, I worked at a diner, and you'll have to wait to see when I die—a short book that would be."

Carly laughed too. "I see what you mean. I guess I will have to create the whole thing."

Nellie said, "Well, if you don't have any more life-changing news to tell me, I better be getting home." She walked to the door and turned to hug Carly. "I surely hope all this works out for you, Carly."

"Thanks, Nellie. Drive safely."

After Nellie left, Carly resumed her place on the sofa with Dinkle at her side. The phone rang.

"Hello."

"Hey, Carly. How's everything?" Thorne asked.

"Oh, just fine. Are you back from your trip?" she asked.

"Yep, just arriving now. Want some company?"

"Sounds great. I haven't thought about supper. Can you pickup Chinese?" Carly suggested.

"Sure. The usual?"

"Yes. I'll see you in a bit."

By the time Thorne arrived, Carly had showered and dressed in her casual white silk blouse and light blue jeans. She found herself thinking of Thorne in a more romantic way. She spoke to Dinkle. "You know, Dink, I believe I care more for Thorne than I have been willing to accept. He's not only a good-looking man, but he seems stable. Also, I feel so secure when he is around. I have come to lean on him more than I ever dreamed."

She looked down at the sincere expression on Dinkle's face and asked, "Do you think I'm right?" Assuming Dinkle agreed, she continued, "Thanks, Dink, I knew you would agree." Passing the mirror, she observed herself one final time for approval and went to the kitchen to set out the plates and silverware. She prepared chamomile and green tea for their meal.

During their dinner, Carly noticed that Thorne seemed preoccupied and asked, "How was your trip? Is anything bothering you? You seem to have something on your mind."

Thorne sipped his tea. "My trip was interesting, and I would say successful."

"That's good." Carly waited for him to explain further.

Thorne pushed his plate away, wiped his mouth with his napkin, and poured them both more tea. "This tea is very good, Carly. I like it better than the tea they serve at the restaurant."

"It's my favorite too. Chamomile is relaxing and green tea is good for you."

Thorne chuckled. "I assume you want me to relax and live a long time."

"You got it." Carly laughed too.

Thorne asked, "Have you given any more thought about finding your bio dad?"

"Not too much." Carly finished her food and sipped her tea. "Nellie came by for lunch today and she asked me about it too, among other things."

"Other things?"

"Yeah, but I'll get to that later. I guess I could forget about the whole business of my real parents. Just get on with my life. But, in another sense, I think I may always wonder how it might have been if I didn't settle it one way or the other."

Thorne cleared his throat and stood. "Let's go into the living room, get more comfortable."

Carly stood. "Do you want more tea?"

"No, I'm fine."

Dinkle squeezed in between the two of them on the sofa. Thorne laughed and rubbed Dinkle on the head.

Carly said, "Thanks for bringing supper. It was good." She took Dinkle from between them and lay her on her other side. "So, back to the subject. Do you think you can find out where my bio dad lives?"

"There are quite a few Joey Saunders in the United States. I will have to do more digging. I'll keep you informed of everything as I find out any information." He was quiet for a moment. "I know the hurt you felt after you contacted Kathleen. More than anything, I want to protect you from further pain. So, I thought about checking it all out before telling you. And, if it was not good, you could be spared. But, as you can see, that wouldn't work. Honesty is the best anyway. I wouldn't want to do anything to hurt our relationship."

Carly looked into his eyes, saw the warm concern he felt. Before she thought, she said, "I love you for that, Thorne."

Thorne took her in his arms, kissed her gently. Carly kissed him back, long and sensual. They held each other, neither spoke for a while. She felt his warm breath on her cheek. Then Thorne said softly, "I love you too, Carly."

Dinkle jumped and barked as if to say, *OK you two, break it up, this is my momma.*

They both laughed. Carly said, "When Nellie was here, she asked about us. She thought there was something between us besides business. Nellie is not the kind of person to beat around the bush, which I guess you have figured out by now."

"Yep, I figured that out when she first called me about finding your birth mom."

Carly stood and picked up Dinkle. "Say goodnight to Thorne. It's your bedtime, sweetie." She took Dinkle to her kennel.

When she returned to the living room, Thorne asked, "Oh yeah, have you listened to Bonnie's tape yet?"

Carly joined him on the sofa. "Yes. I started listening to it today. It's not quite as detailed as I thought it was going to be. Bonnie said she didn't want to relive all her past. She summarized a few things from her early years. Hopefully, I will get another tape soon."

Thorne didn't reply. He reached over and pulled Carly to him, and they enjoyed being close for a long while, not speaking.

Chapter Thirty-Six

Thorne thought about Carly every waking moment during the next day. He relived their times together. Even after all these years, he could not believe he would be able to fall in love with someone after the tragic loss of his wife and baby. But it was happening, and it seemed Carly felt the same for him.

Thorne's search for Joey Saunders wasn't as difficult as he thought it might be. There were six men by that name in the state of North Carolina, a couple were dead, three were the wrong age, and the last one he found to fit the criteria. This Joey Saunders lived on the coast at North Topsail Island. Thorne decided to go see Carly and tell her about finding him.

When he drove past the diner, he saw Carly's car so stopped for lunch. Nellie welcomed him and pointed to Carly seated at the booth at the far end of the diner. When Carly heard Nellie greeting Thorne, she looked around and smiled, and waved him over. He leaned down and kissed her on the cheek.

Carly said, "Mr. Detective, are you stalking me?"

Thorne said, "You can run but you can't hide." They both laughed.

Nellie walked over to take their order, but the diner was so busy she couldn't stay and chat.

Thorne didn't hesitate. "Well, I believe I have found the right Joey Saunders. Of course, you know this could be the wrong one or, for that matter, it may be the right Joey but not your biological father."

Carly shook her head. "I know, Thorne. I really appreciate your efforts, but I know we could be on a wild goose chase."

Thorne said, "What do think about me calling him, giving him a bit of background, etc., and finding out what his reaction is? I mean, it might be better if I find out first because if it is the wrong person, I can keep searching."

Carly broke in and said, "And if it is the right person and he doesn't want me, it will be easier coming from you?"

"Yeah, something like that," Thorne admitted.

Nellie brought their sandwiches and drinks to the booth. "Enjoy. Sorry, I'm so busy. Wish I could join you."

"That's OK, Nellie," Carly said and she turned back to Thorne. "I guess you are right. So, when will you contact him? Will you call him?"

Thorne said, "He works as a contractor and lives at North Topsail Island. So, I thought I would call in the evening to make sure he was home."

Carly asked, "What else do you know about him? Is he married?"

"Yes. He has two grown sons. That's about all."

Carly said, "Oh yeah, I told Nellie about the box and our trip to see Bonnie and her relationship with Kathleen."

"I bet she had a lot of questions."

Carly said, "Not really. She is a dear friend and wants the best for me. I told her I would keep her updated."

Thorne said, "That's good she knows. She has always been there for you." He picked up the check. "Are you going home when you leave here?"

"Not right now. I was on my way to the newspaper office to turn in my article for this week. Also, I need to run by the drugstore to pick up a few things."

"Well, I'll get back to work. I'll call you tonight." Thorne paid the check and walked with Carly to her car. He reached to open the door and paused. "Carly, I can't seem to think about anything but you. I care about you, and I hope beyond hope that this all works out. I would do anything to keep you from being hurt ever again." He put his arm around her shoulders and kissed her softly on her forehead.

Carly looked up at him. "I know that Thorne. I feel so safe and secure with you. No matter how this turns out, it will be OK."

Then he opened her car door and waved as she drove out of the parking lot. As he walked to his car, he noticed that Nellie was not too busy to be looking out the window, and he smiled to himself.

When Carly returned home, she put away her purchases, fixed some lemonade, and sat with Dinkle on the sofa, propped her feet on the coffee table. "What a life!" she said to Dinkle.

Her phone rang, interrupting her thoughts. "Hello."

"Hey, Carly. This is Bonnie."

"Hi, Bonnie. What's up?"

"I think I have good news but wanted to check it out with you."

"Great, what is it?" asked Carly.

"I know I didn't do a very good job on the tape recording. It's really difficult to talk to a machine."

"It was fine. I'm looking forward to more."

"That's what I'm calling about. Josh has signed up for a street festival to sell his art next month in Dunn. That's near you, right?"

"Yes, not far at all."

Bonnie continued. "Well, I thought maybe we could get together, and you could interview me; you know, ask questions. I think I would do better with the story by answering your questions. You could record it if you want, of course. That is, if your schedule allows."

"Wow, that would be fantastic!" exclaimed Carly. "I'm sure I can make plans. What dates next month?"

"It is a three-day show, the second weekend, Friday through Sunday. Josh has a motel booked, so you could come there, or I could come to your house; whatever works best for you."

"Sounds super. We will figure it out. We can talk before then and make a plan."

Bonnie said, "Great. I'll talk to you soon." They hung up.

Carly was excited. This may work out after all. She would make notes about some interview questions to ask Bonnie.

Chapter Thirty-Seven

Thorne picked up the folder with the information about Joey Saunders and dialed the phone.

"Hello," a woman said.

"Hello. Could I speak to Joey Saunders?" Thorne asked.

"I'm sorry, he isn't available right now. Could I give him a message or ask him to return your call?"

Thorne said, "That would be fine. I'd appreciate it." He gave her his name and phone number. "What time do you expect him?"

"It should be within the next hour."

"OK, I'll wait for his call." Thorne hung up. *She sounded rather sophisticated. I hope it's not going to be another bio-mother result.* Thorne took a shower, put on his comfy jogging clothes, got a beer out of the refrigerator, and sat in his easy chair. It wouldn't do any good to try to keep himself occupied because the only thing he could think about was the scenarios of how this might turn out. At about 7:00, the phone rang.

"Hello." Thorne didn't intend to sound so anxious.

The man said, "Is this Thorne Davenport?"

"Yes, it is."

"I'm Joey Saunders. My wife said you called earlier."

"Yes, Mr. Saunders. If you have a few minutes, there is something I would like to discuss with you."

"Concerning?"

"It's a long story, so you might prefer that we talk in person," Thorne suggested.

"I have some time," Joey said. "What's this about?"

Thorne cleared his throat and began. "I guess the best place to start is at the beginning. A few months ago, a lady who lives near Lillington contacted me about locating the biological mother of one of her friends. To shorten that story, I did, and to say the least, that had a very disappointing ending. Since that time, I have talked with that woman's sister about who the biological father might be, and the sister remembered a guy named Joey Saunders who had dated her sister."

Thorne took a breath. "So, the reason for my call is to ask if you might be the right person. The biological mother's name is Kathleen Richardson, her maiden name is Simmons. Are you the Joey that dated her after high school?"

There was a long moment of silence on the phone. Thorne held his breath, waiting for a reply. Finally, he said, "Mr. Saunders, are you still there?"

"Yes, yes, I'm here. I was just taken back a bit, you understand. I mean, we're talking about ancient history practically."

"I realize that a call of this nature and out of the blue can be a pretty big shock," said Thorne.

"Yes, to say the least," Joey Saunders replied.

Thorne asked, "Did you date a girl by that name?"

"Yes, I did. In fact, for quite a few months. But she never told me about any pregnancy. Are you sure of all this?"

"Yes sir, quite sure. I understand if you need some time to think about it," said Thorne.

Joey Saunders said, "No, time won't be necessary. I'm just trying to remember, put a timetable to everything."

"Well, maybe I could help." Thorne continued, "Kathleen dated a guy named Joey Saunders during her last year of high school and during the following summer. She then went to college. Her sister told me that she didn't come home for the holidays. So, we concluded that that was because she didn't want her family to know about the pregnancy and subsequent giving up her baby for adoption."

"Yeah, that's right. I dated Kathleen for that time." A lady's voice was heard in the background. Joey spoke away from the phone and said, "I'll explain when I hang up, Janice." Then he spoke back to Thorne. "That was my wife. I told her I would explain to her later."

Thorne said, "I hope this hasn't caused any problem for you, Mr. Saunders."

"Call me Joey." Joey continued his recall. "After Kathleen went to college, we just drifted apart, as would be expected, I guess. I called her a few times but could tell that the interest had faded. So, we lost contact." Another moment of silence. "You say, I could be this girl's biological father?"

"That's right. I'm sure we could verify it further with DNA testing, if you like."

Joey quickly replied, "Yes, that would be good. I mean, it would do away with any doubts on anyone's part. I think that would be necessary. I'm not denying it, you understand, and I believe it could be possible, but I believe it would be better for all involved to verify it with the testing."

"OK then, I will set up everything and get back to you about where and when the testing will be done."

"That sounds fine." He took a breath. "What is this girl's name? Could you tell me a little about her?"

Thorne wasn't expecting this question. "Her name is Carly Jansen. She is single." *Hopefully not for long,* he thought. "She works as a journalist for a newspaper. She's a sweet person," *and I love her,* he wanted to add.

"I guess I'll learn more when I meet her. You'll call me with the information. I just need to know a couple of days prior so I can make arrangements at work."

"No problem," said Thorne. "I'll be in touch."

Thorne clicked off the phone, looked at his watch. 7:45, it's not too late. I'll go give Carly the news in person. He grabbed his wallet and keys.

Carly heard the doorbell. "Who is it?"

"It's me, Thorne."

She opened the door quickly. "What's wrong?" she asked. "Nothing, not one thing. I just didn't want to call you with the information. Besides, I wanted to see you."

"Information? What? About my dad?"

"Let's sit." He looked around the room. "Where's Dinkle?"

"I have already put him to bed for the night." Thorne smiled, "You mean we're alone!"

"Yes, but my ferocious bodyguard can escape from his kennel if he needs to save me from a raging maniac." They both laughed and Thorne put his arms around her and kissed her.

Carly pulled her head back and looked at Thorne. "Well, are you going to tell me?"

"OK, OK. I think this might not turn out so bad, at least I have my fingers crossed."

"So, you called Joey Saunders?" Carly asked.

"Yes. He wasn't home the first time I called but his wife took my name and number, and he returned my call when he got home from work." They walked over and sat on the sofa. "I told him the highlights of how things have happened up until now, and what I have found out from Kathleen's sister. He was receptive to the whole story. He wasn't angry, belligerent, he didn't hang up on me. And, in the end, he even asked about you, what you are like, etc. I just gave him a brief story, you know, single, sweet journalist, but I left out the most important part of all."

Carly looked at him questioningly. After he didn't speak, she said, "Well, what? The most important part, what is that?"

Without hesitation, Thorne said, "Will you marry me?"

Carly's mouth dropped open. Her eyes wide. "What?"

"Will you marry me?"

Carly answered, "Well right now or in the morning?" They both laughed.

Thorne said, "I know I didn't do this right. No ring, no romantic music or candles, nothing like that. But I'll do it again the right way if you'd rather."

Carly thought. "I'm not real sure all the romantic music, candles, and all that is necessary. Oh, and you forgot about the part where you get on your knees and beg me!"

Thorne kissed her. "I guess it was sudden and totally unexpected, so you can think about it, Carly." He looked at his watch, "Times up!" They laughed again.

Carly sat back on the sofa. "Let me give it some thought, just to be legitimate, OK?"

"That's fine. I totally understand."

"Now, back to the subject at hand. Tell me more about your talk with Joey Saunders."

Thorne replied, "He said that he did date Kathleen around that time and that after she went to college, their relationship cooled and ended. He doesn't doubt the possibility that he could have a daughter but, understandably, he agreed when I suggested DNA testing."

Carly's phone rang.

"Excuse me, Thorne." She reached for the phone. "Hello."

"Is this Carly Jansen?"

"Yes, I'm Carly Jansen."

"Miss Jansen, Nellie Garrett wanted me to call you. I am a nurse at Betsy Johnson Memorial Hospital in Dunn. Nothing to be alarmed about, but we are keeping Ms. Garrett overnight for observation. She wanted you to know."

"What happened?" Carly felt Thorne's hand on her shoulder. "We believe she is suffering from exhaustion, maybe some dehydration as well. Nothing too serious. We're giving her fluids and, like I said, we will observe her overnight. She will most likely go home in the morning."

Carly looked at her watch. It was too late for visiting hours. "May I come see her tonight?"

"Ms. Jansen, our visiting hours are over. She asked me to call and inform you. She made it very clear that she did not want you coming here."

Carly's mind couldn't focus. The shock of Nellie, strong, live forever Nellie, sick? "O, OK. You have to promise that you will call me if anything changes, or she needs me."

"I certainly will. Don't worry, she is doing fine and is in very capable hands."

"Tell her I will see her in the morning, then." Carly hung up.

Thorne asked, "What happened?"

"I'm not sure. The nurse said something about exhaustion and dehydration." She pulled a tissue from the box on the coffee table and blew her nose. "Not Nellie. Nellie is the strongest, most energetic woman I've ever known."

Thorne put his arm around Carly. "You're right and that's why everything will be alright. You'll see."

"I hope you are right, Thorne." She wiped her eyes and leaned back against Thorne. Both were silent for a long while. Then Carly said, "The diner! What should I do about the diner? All the customers will be arriving, and they won't have any idea what is happening."

Thorne said, "No problem. I will go by there on my way home and put a sign on the door. Something like closed due to sickness?"

"I don't know, everyone will be wildly speculating." She thought a while. "Maybe it should read that the diner is closed temporarily, or closed for a week—oh, I don't know."

Thorne said, "You know the sign can always be updated or changed. We can just say closed, reopening next week."

"I guess that would be good. Yeah, that would be OK. Nellie is definitely not going back there until she recuperates fully."

Thorne knew enough about Nellie to know that it would be some miracle if Nellie stayed away that long. "Like you said, Carly, Nellie is a strong willed, energetic, determined kind of woman. A week away from the diner might make her worse."

"I know. That's like her home." Thorne stood. "It's time I get going."

She followed him to the door. He turned to her. "Carly, you are going to think about my question, right?"

It took Carly a second to remember the question. "I will. I think I already know my answer." She looked up at Thorne and whispered, "I love you too." The kiss and embrace would not soon be forgotten by either of them.

"I'll call you tomorrow. Let me know how Nellie's doing."

"I plan to be at the hospital first thing. I'll let you know."

"Bye for now."

Carly watched him drive away. She knew he was the one she wanted to be with forever. She went back inside. Sleep was the farthest thing from her mind.

Chapter Thirty-Eight

The next morning, Carly had just gotten dressed when her doorbell rang. She called out, "Who is it?"

"Your future husband!"

She opened the door and almost jumped into his arms. Thorne said, "What's wrong? Is everything OK?"

"Yes, nothing's wrong. I'm just glad to see you."

"Well, now I can get used to a greeting like that every day." They walked inside. "I thought I would drive you to the hospital. Have you heard any news?"

"No. I guess everything is OK. But I still want to go." Dinkle came through the doggie door to greet Thorne. Carly asked, "Have you had any breakfast? Want coffee?"

"No thanks. I'm fine. I'm ready if you are."

Thorne tuned the radio to the a.m. talk station. Thorne wanted to ask if she had made her mind up about marrying him but knew this wasn't the best time. Besides, maybe he would do the romantic thing, dinner, a ring, and of course, down on one knee.

When they arrived at the Nellie's room, she was dressed, ready to be checked out. Against Nellie's wishes to return to the diner, Thorne took her to Carly's. As they got out of the car, Thorne said, "You ladies behave. No skydiving or running the hundred-yard dash." They all laughed.

Carly blew him a kiss. "Come on Nellie. I'll fix you some lemonade or tea and you can just take it easy this afternoon."

Nellie followed Carly and obediently sat on the sofa. Dinkle jumped up to see what was wrong. "Hey Dink. You know Nellie's fine, right? Just tell your Mamma that I don't need a babysitter, OK?"

Carly brought the lemonade and sat in the chair near the patio door. "You scared me to death, Nellie. You aren't supposed to get sick; you know that right?"

Nellie waved her hand. "I'm not sick, never have been, really. When Ezra came to the diner; you've never met him, I don't think. Anyway, he saw me leaning on the counter, looking a little pale, I guess, and he called the ambulance." She took a drink of lemonade. "Um, that's refreshing," and placed her glass on the coffee table. "Anyway, I didn't have enough energy to argue. I was just tired from the busy day. No big deal. But you know doctors, they must test for everything. I've been poked and prodded so much I feel like a pincushion."

"Don't you worry one bit. Thorne put up a sign to let people know you are closed for a few days."

Nellie said, "I appreciate your concern, but I'm fine, really. Besides, I can't just sit around all day, I will be sick. I need to be at the diner. I'll take it a little easier, I promise." Then, as usual, getting right to the point, Nellie said, "Saw you and Thorne kissing in the parking lot the other day. So, want to tell me what's going on with you two?"

Carly blushed. "You want some more lemonade?"

"Quit changing the subject. Now tell me. Has he proposed yet?"

Carly couldn't hide the excited expression. "Well, in fact, he sort of did."

"Sort of did?"

"I think it was a slip of the tongue during a happy moment. He certainly had not planned it very well."

"What do you mean?"

Carly started explaining. "First, let me tell you that Thorne found Joey Saunders. He called him and had a great reception. Joey agreed to a DNA test just to verify everything." Carly looked at Nellie. "Let me get you a blanket, Nellie. You can lie back on the sofa and rest a bit."

"Might as well. Now tell me, when is this DNA test going to be done? And tomorrow I'm going back to the diner."

"OK Nellie, you win. I'll take you to the diner early in the morning, but I'm going to help you, at least for the lunch crowd. No argument. It is the way it's going to be. I don't know about the test yet. Thorne will let me know."

"I have a good feeling about all this. You are a dear, my sweet girl and sure deserve good things."

Thorne knew he had to plan a more romantic, appropriate proposal for Carly. He gave it quite a bit of thought and decided just what he would do and made the plans.

When he got to his office the next morning, his cell phone rang. "Carly, hi."

"Are you busy?"

"Yes, sure, I'm always too busy to talk to you."

"Oh, you." Carly laughed. "I just wanted to tell you that I'm here at the diner with Nellie and I'm going to help her with the lunch hour before going to the newspaper office."

"I see Nellie won the fight."

"She's definitely a determined one."

Chapter Thirty-Nine

The next week, when he got to his office, the DNA results had been delivered. He considered waiting to open the envelope until he was with Carly, but his impatience won. He poured himself a cup of coffee and sat down at his desk, looked at the envelope and picked up the letter opener. He called Carly and they planned to have dinner that evening. He didn't want to tell her about receiving the DNA, not knowing the result, and especially not over the phone.

When Carly got home from the diner that afternoon, she was so tired that she and Dinkle took a nap on the sofa. Carly's doorbell woke her.

"Who is it?"

"It's me, Thorne Davenport, your personal private investigator." When she opened the door, "You know, I need to get you a key. This is a little ridiculous, you having to knock every time you visit."

"No problem." Thorne held out the envelope. Carly's eyes widened. "The results."

"Just tell me, Thorne. Is he the one?"

"You can see for yourself. Open it. You might want to sit down."

"Is it bad?" she asked. They went to the kitchen, and she pulled out the paper. Her hands were a little shaky. When she read the results, she just stood still, paralyzed from disbelief, fear and a million other feelings. She sat at the bar. "Oh my. Thorne, this is real? There's no mistake?"

"DNA is pretty dang accurate." He stood closer to her and put his arm around her shoulder. "Now all we have to do is let Joey Saunders know he has a grown daughter."

Tears filled Carly's eyes. "I'm scared Thorne. What if—"

Thorne pulled her up from the bar stool and held her. He whispered, "It's going to be just fine, Carly. I really believe that. You'll see."

Dinkle was sitting at Carly's feet, looking up with concern. "It's OK, girl."

Thorne asked, "How was the work at the diner today? Did Nellie behave or did she try to do everything?"

"I think we worked together well. I tried to do most of the walking back and forth to tables. I tell you one thing; I do not see how Nellie could do that every day. When I got home, I was so exhausted I had to take a nap."

"Like you said, Nellie is one tough lady," Thorne said. "Now, about your dad. Do you want to call him or should I?"

"Well, Mr. My Private Detective, since you've done such a super job, I think you should continue to work things out."

"OK, but my price needs to triple, you understand?"

Carly loved his sense of humor. Thorne said, "OK, I'll contact him and go from there." He leaned down to pet Dinkle. "OK, Dink, you take care of things. I've got to get going."

"I wish you didn't have to go. I could fix us a salad for supper."

"No, I really need to get going. I'll talk to you tomorrow." He kissed her sincerely. "I love you, Carly."

On the way home, Thorne thought about a romantic occasion to formally ask Carly to marry him. He decided that an intimate dinner at his house would be the best. Tomorrow he would buy the engagement ring and plan the dinner on Friday night.

Chapter Forty

The next day, Thorne called Joey and informed him of the DNA test results. The man was excited.

"That's wonderful. My wife and I have discussed it and we will be very happy to welcome her into our family."

Thorne was so relieved. He knew Carly would be overjoyed.

Joey continued, "Listen, Thorne, we want Carly to visit us at our home, heck, for that matter, stay with us a while, you know, so we can get to know her and her us."

Thorne said, "You can't imagine how happy I am to hear this. I will give the news to Carly, and she will call you to make any plans."

"I appreciate all you've done for her. Is there any payment for your services? I will be glad to cover them."

"No, no, it's all covered. I appreciate your offer, though." They hung up.

Thorne called Carly and gave her the news and Joey's phone number. "It will be fine, Carly. Just call when you feel like it. He invited you to visit or even stay with them for a while, to get to know each other."

"I can't believe it," Carly exclaimed.

"Well, it's true. I couldn't be happier for you." He continued, "Speaking of true and happy, I am inviting you out Friday night for a special dinner."

"This Friday?" Carly asked.

"Yes, I'll pick you up around 4 o'clock. Is that good for you?" Carly knew that she didn't have any plans and said, "Yes, that will be fine. What should I wear?"

"Nothing?" Thorne stated.

"You are silly. No, really, where are we going?"

"That will be a surprise. Just wear casual, anything really."

"OK, I'll see you Friday about 4 o'clock."

Thorne remembers, "Oh yes, Joey's wife's name is Janice. See you Friday."

Carly went by the diner on her way to the newspaper office. She told Nellie about the dinner Thorne had planned for Friday. "He's going to pick me up."

Nellie said, with I *bet I know what he has planned look on her face.* "Sounds interesting. Wonder what he's up to?" She smiled mischievously.

"Oh Nellie, you are such a romantic," Carly remembered she hadn't told Nellie about Joey's response to Thorne's call. So, she gave her the details. Of course, Nellie was overjoyed for her and gave her a hug.

When Carly returned home from the newspaper office, she decided to call Joey. A woman answered. "Hello."

"Hello." Carly felt a huge lump in her throat. "Is this Mrs. Saunders?"

"Yes, may I ask who is calling?"

"Ms. Saunders, my name is Carly Jansen and—"

Janice didn't give her time to finish. "Oh, Carly, it is so wonderful that you called. We can't wait to meet you. We feel like we've been blessed. How are you, my dear?"

"I'm fine. To tell you the truth, I was a little apprehensive about calling even though Thorne reassured me that it was alright."

"Absolutely, my dear. Hold on, let me get Joey."

Carly heard her call out to Joey. He took the phone. "Hello, hello, Carly?"

"Yes, it's me." She felt like she would faint. Her mind went blank, her mouth was dry as cotton.

"Listen, Carly, don't you worry about anything. We are so happy to hear from you and can't wait to meet you. We must plan to get together very soon if that's OK with you."

"Yes, I'd like that." Carly managed to speak.

Joey continued. "We live at North Topsail Island. I believe that is a little over two hours from where you live."

Carly thought, *That's not very far.* She thought about Thorne taking her and said, "Joey, I hope it's alright if Thorne comes too. He can drive."

"Should have thought of that myself, sorry. But yes, he is certainly invited. I mean, without him, we wouldn't have you."

"Let me see when he can make it and I'll call you back to settle on the best time for you and your wife too."

"Sounds like a plan," Joey answered. "I am so looking forward to it. Plan to stay as long as you like."

"I will and I look forward to it as well," Carly said and they hung up.

Chapter Forty-One

Thorne quit work early Friday to get the house in order. The caterer would arrive at 6:30. He was picking up old newspapers, books, his socks, and a few other items lying around. He looked at the mantel where some CDs were scattered. He saw the framed photo of his wife and stopped. He picked up the frame, felt sadness, and said aloud, "My sweetness, I have missed you every single moment since you've been gone. I know you would want me happy. His eyes teared up. I have found a wonderful woman that I plan to marry but I will always love you in my deepest soul."

He took the photo and put it on the top of his closet, where he had other memories of their time together.

Thorne arrived at Carly's house about four o'clock Friday afternoon. She was dressed casually, in tan slacks, a lavender silk blouse, and leather sandals. It was about a 20-minute drive to Thorne's house.

"Where are we going?" asked Carly.

"You'll see," said Thorne.

He pulled the car into his driveway. Carly said, "So, this is where you live?"

"Yes, lady, welcome to my humble abode." They went inside. "I made your favorite chamomile tea; would you like a cup?"

"Yes, that would be nice."

Carly wondered about his plan. Thorne read her mind and said, "The caterers will be at 6:30."

"Caterers?" she asked.

"Yes, I know you like healthy and I'm not exactly a healthy cook, so I ordered our dinner. I believe you will like it."

They talked a bit about various subjects. Carly remembered and said, "I forgot to tell you about all the happenings with Joey. But Bonnie called me and said that Josh is selling his art at a street festival next month; it's a three-day show. She explained how she felt about talking to a tape recorder and thought it might be better if I interview her, ask specific questions."

Thorne said, "I can understand. I think it would be difficult to talk to a machine. Do you know what kind of questions you will ask?"

"Not really. I think I'll play it by ear. See how the conversation goes. I'm sure one thing will lead to another and so on."

Thorne looked at his watch. "The caterer should be here soon. Hope you are hungry."

"I am."

He led Carly to the dining table where he lit candles. There were plates with flower designs on them, nice silverware, and China teacups. Thorne said, "I thought tea would be better, since you are not that fond of wine."

"You already know me so well," she said as she sat in the chair that he pulled out for her.

Thorne said in a formal voice, "Excuse me, mam, I shall return momentarily." He went to open the door for the caterer.

After their meal of seafood delicacies, Thorne poured another cup of tea. He brought from the kitchen the ring box, went to Carly, knelt on one knee, opened the ring box, and looked into her eyes. "Carly Jansen, I want you to be with me forever and I'm asking if you will be my wife."

The smile on Carly's face lit up the whole room. "Oh, Thorne, you are the only man I have ever loved. I trust you. I feel safe with you. I would love more than anything to be your wife."

Thorne took the ring from the box and slid it onto her ring finger. He stood, lifted Carly from her chair, and held her, looking into her eyes. They held each other. Both had happy tears in their eyes.

Chapter Forty-Two

Carly couldn't wait to call Nellie the next morning. Nellie answered, "Green Hornet Grill."

Carly blurted, "You'll never guess!"

Nellie said, "OK, why don't you just tell me?"

"Last night he proposed. After we had a delicious meal, he got on his knees, the whole thing. It was wonderful."

"Girl, girl, I am sooooo happy for you, and Thorne too."

"I felt like I was dreaming. Also, another good thing is I called Joey. His wife, Janice answered. They really sound like good people. I already feel welcome, even though I'm nervous about going there."

Nellie asked, "Is Thorne going too?"

"Yes, he will drive. They wanted him to come as well."

Nellie asked, "Will I see you today? I must see your ring!"

"I'm not sure if I'll make it there today. I need to get ready for our trip to see Joey. We talked about it last night. Thorne called them and we are going next Saturday. It's only about a two-hour drive. I feel a little nervous, even though they made me feel very welcome, just like a member of the family."

"Well, you are, my dear. I'm glad they included Thorne."

Carly said, "We'll tell them when we see them about Thorne becoming their son-in-law."

Nellie said, "I knew everything would work out, Carly. Customers are coming in, so, I'll talk to you later, OK?"

"Sure, Nellie. Later."

Chapter Forty-Three

Joey and Janice Saunders welcomed Carly and Thorne with open arms. Joey said, "Come on out back to the porch. I'm grilling some hamburgers." The balcony porch overlooked the ocean.

"This is a beautiful scene," Carly said. "I can imagine having my tea here every morning; what a peaceful way to start the day."

Janice replied, "You are right, Carly. I spend a lot of my mornings out here most of the year. Of course, there are times the seas are rough, strong winds blow, but even inside, it is an awesome view."

Carly said, "It makes me feel small, yet significant somehow."

Janice and Carly prepared the fixings in the kitchen. Joey finished the burgers and brought them to the inside table as the wind was up. During their meal, they made small talk. Joey had quite a sense of humor and told jokes, which made them laugh. After they finished eating, Carly offered to help with the dishes.

Janice said, "No way, my dear. These dishes will be here tomorrow. We want to spend all the time with you."

Carly replied, "Me too. I can't believe how wonderful you and Joey have been to me, and Thorne too."

Janice said, "Carly, I'm so sorry that your birth mom treated you the way she did. I know it must have been devastating for you."

Carly said, "It was. At first, I couldn't believe it, but after some time and sorting through my feelings, I'm adjusting to the fact that she never wanted me." Then she asked, "Do you have any children?"

"We have two sons: Keith, who is married to Marie, and Roger who is married to Patsy. Neither have children."

Janice wanted to ask if Carly wanted children but decided just to wait and see. After a moment, Janice said, "Come on, let's join Joey and Thorne in the den."

The den was more like a sunroom. The view was awesome. Joey broke the silence. "Well, Carly, since we don't have a lot of time, can you tell us all about your life in thirty minutes?" They all laughed.

"Sure," Carly said. "I lived 34 years and found my second family." Tears came to her eyes. Thorne put his hand on her arm.

Thorne added, "And I have more good news. Carly and I are engaged to be married."

Janice clapped and said, "Oh my, a daughter and son, all at one time!"

Joey lifted his coffee. "Cheers, to the newlyweds. May you love and cherish each other forever."

They all raised their cups. "Here, here."

Joey said, "You should have your wedding here, on the beach."

Janice said, "Great idea! Oh, it would be so exciting."

Joey added, "You don't have to worry about anything. Janice and I will plan the whole event. Invite all your friends. What do you think?"

Carly thought about her friends in Lillington and knew they would want to come. Then she thought, I have a dad. She didn't know if she wanted to cry or laugh from happiness. After more discussion, it was decided that the wedding would be in mid-September on the beach. Although the visit was short, Carly and Thorne both felt at home.

It was getting late, so Carly asked Thorne, "Are you ready to go home?"

"If you are. I'm on your clock."

Joey said, "I hope a day doesn't go by that we don't hear from Carly. I know you are busy with your life, but maybe we could keep in touch, at least by texting during the busy times."

"No problem," said Carly. "I look forward to it."

Carly and Thorne were mostly quiet on the way home, each with their thoughts of the day.

Dinkle was waiting anxiously when Carly arrived home.

Carly continued her human-interest stories for the newspaper, although with effort because all she could think about was her upcoming wedding. Nellie agreed to close the diner that Saturday since she was to be Carly's Maid of Honor.

Chapter Forty-Four

The art show in Dunn was to begin Friday, so Carly went to the grocery store and bought food to prepare for Bonnie's visit. She made sure she had paper and pens and cassettes for their visit. She hoped they got a lot of topics covered but had no idea how it would go.

Thorne called. "Hey, my soon-to-be wife! Are you ready for Bonnie's visit?"

Carly said, "Yes, I've been to the grocery store. I have no idea what Bonnie likes to eat, so I bought different things and hope there is something she will want."

Thorne asked, "What time will she arrive?"

"You know, I'm not sure. We didn't talk about that. I'll call her and get the details. I know the show is in Dunn and I assume she will ride with Josh. Let me call her and I'll let you know."

Thorne said, "If I can help, let me know."

"OK, I will."

Carly called Bonnie. "Hey, Bonnie. Thorne and I were just talking. Do you know what time you will be here?"

Bonnie said, "Josh has to be at the show early, about 6:30. Is that too early for you?"

"No problem at all. Listen, instead of Josh having to come by here, I'll ask Thorne to pick you up. He lives in Dunn, so no problem. That way Josh can go straight there. Is that alright?"

"That would be great. I appreciate that and I'm sure Josh will like it too. He gets so anxious before a show."

"I understand," said Carly. "I'll talk to Thorne and call you back if anything changes. I would say he can pick you up around 7 o'clock Friday morning."

"I really appreciate it. I'm looking forward to our visit." Carly called Thorne and all was set.

Chapter Forty-Five

That Friday, Thorne drove to Main Street but found that he had to park on a side street as the Main Street was blocked for the festival. He walked down the street; all the vendors were busy setting up their displays. He spotted Bonnie and went to her.

"Bonnie," he called.

"Oh hey, Thorne. Come meet Josh."

Josh was busy unpacking boxes but turned and shook hands with Thorne.

Thorne said, "I know you are busy, Josh. Hope we can get together later."

"Yes," Josh said. "Good to meet you. Bonnie told me about your and Carly's visit. Sorry, I wasn't there. And, yes, it's quite a job setting up my tables and display. I better get back to it."

"I understand. Good luck in the show," said Thorne, and he looked at Bonnie. "You ready to go?"

"Yes," Bonnie said bye to Josh, and he nodded his reply.

They walked back to Thorne's car. "Carly is looking forward to your visit."

"Me too, I think," Bonnie said.

They drove up to Carly's house. Thorne said, "I hope Carly told you about her ferocious guard dog."

"She told me that he was a Yorkie mix."

"Yes, but he is jealous of our getting too close to one another." He smiled. "He's quite a baby really, and spoiled rotten, I might add."

Bonnie said, "I love my dogs too. They are like my children."

Carly opened the door as they walked up to the porch. "Come in, come in."

Thorne paused and said, "I know you girls have a lot to talk about and I need to get to work." He gave Carly a quick kiss. "Have fun. Call me if I can do anything, OK?"

"I will, Thorne, and thanks a million."

Carly went inside, closed the door. "Bonnie, I want you to make yourself at home. I bought different kinds of snacks and things we can fix for lunch. I hope there is something you like. You just feel free to eat whatever you find. We can decide on lunch later."

Bonnie followed Carly into her living room. "I've got everything ready. I know you have a lot to tell, so we can get started anytime." She said, "I will sit on the sofa. You might like the chair near the patio doors. It's a small yard but a nice view. One of the nice things about this house is that it is quiet, no busy street or city noises."

Bonnie said, "That's what I like about our house too, although we hear some cars at times, it's only nature sounds for the most part." Before sitting, she said to Carly, "You said to make myself at home, so I sure would like some coffee."

"Of course, there is a pot on the kitchen counter and mugs are hanging on the wall behind it. Feel free to get it. I remembered you like honey, so it is on the counter as well and, of course, milk is in the refrigerator."

Bonnie went to the kitchen to get some coffee. "Can I get you anything, Carly?

"No, I'm fine. I have some tea I made myself earlier."

Bonnie came back to the living room, sat her coffee cup on the table beside her chair. She said, "That was so sweet of Thorne to pick me up. Josh really appreciated it too." She sipped her coffee. "You know, I've done a lot of thinking since we decided to do this. I've tried to think of good and happy times, not just the bad times."

Carly said, "I hope you don't mind, but I would like to tape this. I also will make notes for myself as we go along."

"No problem. Where do you want me to begin?"

"Anywhere you like," Carly replied.

Bonnie sipped her coffee. "I will probably need to take quite a few cigarette breaks today."

"That's fine. I don't have any ashtrays, but I'll get an empty food can for you to use."

"OK. I guess I'll start. On the tape I sent you, I told you a little about my early years. I can't remember exactly what I included, so I might repeat myself."

"No problem," Carly reassured her. "I won't interrupt unless I have a question, OK?"

Bonnie began. "Like I said, I've been trying to think of good things. I remember my dad used to read to us, my sister and me. My brother was born twelve years after me, so growing up, it was just myself and Kate. He read *O'*

Captain, My Captain, The Raven, and my favorite was a poem that one of his black professors at Campbell College wrote. It was called, *Ho d' Wus Ro Fus— and soon in d' mawnin.*

"Later, when I was learning calligraphy, I wrote it for him and framed it, and gave it to him for Christmas. There were many more that I can't recall. He also had a couple of songs he sang, I guess from his childhood. *It was Midnight on the Ocean, not a streetcar was in sight.* I can't remember all the words unless I sing it—believe me, you don't need that recorded." Bonnie laughed and sipped her coffee, then continued. "I do, however, remember the words to the other one, *The Hole in the Bottom of the Sea.*"

Carly said, "Can you say the words to it?"

"I think so, let me try." Bonnie started in a sing-song rhythm.

There's a hole in the bottom of the sea. Oh, that hole, that beautiful hole, there's a hole in the bottom of the sea.

There's a log on the hole in the bottom of the sea. Oh, that hole that beautiful hole. There's a hole in the bottom of the sea.

There's a frog on the log in the hole at the bottom of the sea. Oh, that hole, that beautiful hole, there's a hole in the bottom of the sea.

There's a dress on the frog on the log on the hole in the bottom of the sea. Oh, that hole, that beautiful hole. There's a hole in the bottom of the sea.

There's a needle in the dress on the frog on the log on the hole in the bottom of the sea. Oh, that hole, that beautiful hole. There's a hole in the bottom of the sea.

There's a thread in the needle in the dress on the frog on the log on the hole in the bottom of the sea. Oh, that hole. That beautiful hole. There's a hole in the bottom of the sea.

There's a knot in the thread in the needle in the dress on the frog on the log on the hole in the bottom of the sea. Oh, that hole. That beautiful hole. There's a hole in the bottom of the sea.

Bonnie took a break, sipped her coffee. "You sing it faster and faster. My dad could sing it fast. It took me a while to get it all straight. Anyway, that is one of my good memories. My dad also taught me to ride a bicycle without training wheels. He held on to the seat and walked fast beside me. When he knew I had it, he let go and I had the confidence to do it on my own. He also helped me with math problems. He would draw the three apples, erase one and so I knew that three minus one was two. That's just a simple example but it made math visual to me."

Carly asked, "Did your mom help you with homework or anything?"

Bonnie said, "No. One thing I remember that was good is that she made some clothes for our Ginny Doll in a case. My case was blue, my sister's pink. At Christmas, the colors were always blue for me, pink for Kate. I guess Kate was prissier than I was; I was more of a tomboy. Mom did the devotions every night. She would read something out of the Bible, and we would say our prayers. The prayer was *Now I lay me down to sleep. I pray the Lord my soul to keep. If I should die before I wake, I pray the Lord my soul to take.* Now that I think about it, I think that part about dying in your sleep still haunts me."

Bonnie half smiled. "I guess you've noticed that I'm not fond of hugging. I used to cringe when my mother would hug me. It seemed to me that she was consoling herself somehow.

"I can't think of that many good things about my mother. She was the disciplinarian. She did the punishing and I have to say, I felt that I got the brunt of it. Most of the time, I was innocent or taken wrongly. I could tell that my sister was sad for me when I got a whipping. Sometimes I had to bend over the commode, and she would whip me with the belt, or a switch from outside. She always seemed so mad when she would do this. I still feel that way today.

"Over time, I grew to fear her. My dad was always at work, so he didn't really know about this. The thing I didn't like was that my mother could whip me and tell me that it hurt her more than it did me and that she loved me. That may explain my misunderstanding of love for most of my life." Bonnie looked out through the patio doors.

"I think I told you on the tape about my piano lessons. Well, I liked playing the piano and had lessons for five years. My teacher entered me in a competition every year, and I got a gold, silver, or bronze lapel pin, according to the number of pieces I played. I had a talent for adding my own notes to the songs I played. Although my lessons were all classical music, I was the best at church songs. I played in church for my sister to sing. My mother sang alto, my sister sang soprano. I always got praised for playing the piano. My dad would sit in the chair at home after supper and fall asleep listening to me play.

"Sometime around 1970, I met a lady at the church I went to. Her name is Millie. She was Italian and full of spunk. She decided that I was going to be a concert pianist. Of course, that was one of my dreams as a girl. Even though my home life was a disaster, she saw the plan through. I had a piano concert at a local high school. I was so nervous. I had to use the written sheet music because I couldn't memorize all the songs. Quite a few people came.

"My sister, Kate, sang a solo, *Songbird* by *Fleetwood Mac*. For a finale, I played the *Warsaw Concerto*. The performance was far from perfect, but I was happy. A long-playing album was recorded. My sister's song wasn't on the album, I assume because of copyright issues. Millie did a professional job. There was a write-up in the newspaper about it, as well as my happy home life. I knew that to be a concert pianist you had to practice every day for many hours and I knew I would not like that part.

"Another thing I remember is when my mother would go somewhere, maybe choir practice, or a Tupperware party, dad would let us watch television. I loved that. But, when mom came home, it was TV off and to bed. So, the shows were ended prematurely. So, I learned not to like TV that much. I did enjoy the 'The Fugitive' with David Jansen; not much else. On Saturdays, when we were little, we could watch a few cartoons, *Popeye* mainly, *Sky King*, and *The Lone Ranger*. Then we had to go outside and play for most of the rest of the day. Sometimes the neighborhood kids would come over. We would play store or school; I was always the store owner and schoolteacher. When we got older, we had to do house chores, which had to be repeated if they were done good enough."

After a few minutes of quiet, Carly said, "Let's take a break, Bonnie. You want a snack?" They walked to the kitchen, fixed crackers and cheese and olives. Carly asked, "Does Josh do many art shows?"

"Yes, about one every month, when the weather is nice. He has a tent he uses when it's necessary. He does better at some shows than others. It tires him out because he likes his solitude and dealing with all those people is far from that."

When they finished their snack, they returned to the living room and Bonnie asked, "Do you think I'm telling too many details, Carly?"

"Not at all. The more the better. It gives me a sense of the real picture as well as your feelings about things."

"So, where was I?" Bonnie asked.

"Piano playing, singing in church, playing outside."

"OK. Besides piano, I played the xylophone and clarinet in my high school band. We played at football games and in the Christmas parade. When I was in the fourth grade, I believe it was, I was a majorette in the Christmas parade down Main Street. Let me tell you, I nearly froze to death. I never got good at baton twirling but did OK."

Carly asked, "On the tape, you told me about the swing falling on your head. Any other injuries?"

"I broke my left arm when playing softball. I can't remember how old I was. Earlier than that, I slammed my thumb on the car door. We had a 1957 Ford Mercury. I wanted to beat my sister to the car, so I got in and pulled the door shut fast, and my left hand was in the area where the door slammed on me when it closed. That is not a good memory at all. The man in the ER practically had to sew my thumb back on." Bonnie shivered at the thought.

"When that swing fell on my head, the medical people didn't seem to know much about head injuries back then, so besides watching for symptoms of a concussion, nothing was done. Personally, I believe that changed my personality somewhat. At least, that's what I think, looking back." Bonnie paused, then said, "I think I'll take a cigarette break, Carly."

"Let me get that can for you." Carly went to the trashcan in the kitchen, rinsed out the can, and brought it to Bonnie.

"Thanks." Bonnie went outside and walked around the yard.

When she returned, she poured herself another cup of coffee and sat in her chair. "OK, now, where was I?"

Carly changed the cassettes in the recorder and labeled the first one.

Carly said, "You said on your tape that things changed when you were about 14."

"Yes, I became rebellious, at least toward my mother. I had started writing in a diary, one I got for Christmas when I was 13. It was my secret place; I could say anything. Not that there were that many secrets until later.

"One summer, I went to our church camp in Tacoa Falls, Georgia. Our preacher's son at that time, Johnny, was my true love, I knew. I didn't know anything about hormones or sex, or relationships with the opposite sex. The only thing my mother ever told me was to never let a boy touch you, which she told me quite a few times.

"At camp that summer, Johnny and I walked to the falls. He was taller than me, so I stood on a rock near the falls so I could be the same height as he was.

He kissed me, on the lips, dry, soft, rather quickly. I felt warm all over and so excited. I knew I had found true love. We walked back to the dorms at camp and that was that. When I was older, I dreamed of Johnny coming to the door and saving me like some white knight on a horse.

"When I went to Junior High, our bus driver, Bruce, was a senior at the high school. I thought he was so cute, short, olive complexion, brown hair, and nice hands. I looked forward to seeing him every day. I can't recall the details, but one day, I skipped school with him. I had never skipped school. We went to his house. His parents weren't home.

"I was nervous but he reassured me. He kissed me and his hands touched places that I knew were wrong. I was so scared I would be pregnant. He reassured me. It seemed he knew what he was doing. Well, long story short, I was no longer a virgin. The principal at school had called my parents about me not being at school.

"Truancy was a serious matter back then. My dad came to Bruce's house and, oh boy, that was not a good day. When I got home and went to my room, my dad came in and, to my shock, he slapped my face. I guess he was at his wits' end and so exasperated he couldn't hold it in any longer.

"Sometime after that, I came home from school one day; my mother was ironing clothes in the kitchen. As soon as I walked in the door, she ordered me not to see or talk to Bruce ever again. She had found out from one of the neighbors that he was a drunk and that his family was no good as well.

"I was so tired of her ordering me around. Little did she know that the same day I had already broken up with Bruce because I found out that he drank. Well, after she gave me the order, I changed my mind out of rebellion. So, the next day, Bruce and I were back going steady—that's what it was called back then.

"That summer, around July 4, we secretly met at the elementary school nearby. Bruce told me that he had joined the Navy and would be leaving for boot camp soon. I let my emotions control my mind that day. Besides, he needed me, at least that's what he said.

"That summer I started a part-time job working in the laboratory at the local hospital. I would draw blood from patients and run the lab tests. After I missed my period, I ran a urine pregnancy test on myself, under a fake name, of course. It returned positive. I was at a total loss of what to do. I was scared beyond all reasoning. Of course, I wrote this in my diary.

"Sometime later, near the end of summer, I was asleep on a Sunday morning and my mother entered my room and sat on the side of my bed. She asked if I had anything to tell her. I said no, of course. To this day, I hate it when people ask a question that they already know the answer to, just to try and trick me. I never read anything private that my children had. They could leave a personal letter or anything else in view and I would not read it.

"Anyway, my mother told me what she knew and how things were going to be from now on. Bruce's parents came over and met with my parents and they planned my future. I was in the room but had no say in the matter. Bruce would be home from basic training on September 8 and we would be married on September 9, 1966, Friday night, at the church.

"I do remember meeting with the preacher, Rev. Hagar. He was a kind man. He said that one sin is no bigger in God's sight than another. The difference was the results of the situation here on earth. This I already was aware of and learned even more about as time passed." Bonnie paused, a little out of breath, and said, "I think I'll take a two cigarette break now, Carly."

Carly shook her head. Her mind was full of thoughts and her feelings were engrossed in Bonnie's story. She went to the kitchen and drank a glass of water. Bonnie came back inside.

Back in the living room, Carly changed the cassette again. She said, "I know this is difficult for you, Bonnie. I find it extremely interesting. We can stop anytime you want."

"Not yet," said Bonnie. "I'd just as soon finish today, if possible."

"Sounds good, but remember, you can stop anytime."

"OK." Bonnie sipped her coffee and continued, "The next thing I remember is the night of the wedding. I was in a light blue knee-length Sunday dress, I think a flower in my hair and a small bouquet in my hands. I was standing in a little room off the foyer in the church. There was a little voice inside me that wanted to run, to holler I don't want to do this. But I kept quiet about my fear and anxiety.

"There were no people at my wedding, as no one was invited. It was just his parents, my parents, the organ player, and the preacher, of course. I was in a fog, can't remember the details, just the fact that I was not doing what I wanted to do."

Carly interrupted. "Were you given the choice of adoption or abortion?"

"Are you kidding? Back then? No way. And, besides, I dreamed my whole life of being a mother, a wife, and having a wonderful life. I could make that dream come true; I just knew it. Anyway, after the wedding, we went to his parents' house. He immediately went to visit some of his buddies. His mother was nice to me, but I didn't really feel at home. I had my own bedroom. I spent most of that weekend alone.

"The next week, Bruce had to return to go overseas. I got homesick, not to return home, but just to be out of this strange place. I was still working at the hospital, second shift, 3-11 o'clock. Bruce's mother worked the same shift at McPherson Eye Hospital as an aid. We would get home at the same time each night, watch a little late TV talk show, and she would laugh a lot. We both smoked. Yes, I started smoking earlier.

"To go back in time, when I was young, I snuck a cigarette from my Papa, a non-filter Chesterfield, I think, and smoked it. Never coughed or anything. I liked it. When I was a teenager and babysat for one of our neighbors, I smoked, blowing the smoke out of the bathroom window while the girl I was babysitting watched *Batman* on TV.

"Anyway, back to the story. I gradually became accustomed to my new life at Bruce's parents' house. A little morning sickness was all I had. Bruce was still away; he wouldn't return until April the next year, 1967. At Christmas, Bruce's dad got so drunk that he fell into the Christmas tree, and I put it back together. I really didn't like my situation.

"In February of the next year, my parents helped me buy a cute little house, not far from them. I was so excited. I made it beautiful. I was getting very excited to start my dream of being the perfect and loving wife and having my children and living happily ever after."

Carly interrupted. "Did you still go to church?"

"No, I didn't. The people seemed to judge me and look down on me. I anxiously waited for Bruce to return from overseas. On March 31, 1967, my Melanie was born. I hated the doctor; she was cold, harsh, and rough. I don't know what her problem was, but she was in the wrong profession, in my opinion.

"When I held Melanie in my arms, the tears came, my heart filled with more love than one would think possible. I had never known this overwhelming feeling of devotion and protectiveness. I was a good mother. I loved rocking her, singing *You Are My Sunshine* to her. She was the most precious thing in the entire world. I couldn't wait for Bruce to see her and experience this love." Bonnie got up, "I'll be right back," and walked outside to have a cigarette.

Carly thought about the journals in the box and knew something had gone terribly wrong.

Bonnie returned. "Are you tired yet, Carly?"

"No, I'm fine and I must say mesmerized by your life. It's almost lunch. Let's take a lunch break and we can resume after that."

"Sounds good."

Chapter Forty-Six

After lunch and a cigarette, Bonnie resumed telling her story. "Bruce was due home, and I was so excited. He came in on a Friday. He didn't come home until he had visited his parents and some friends. When he did get home, he was drunk. He didn't seem all that happy to see me, his house, or his daughter. He quickly got extremely mad, started yelling at me like I had taken control of him and everything in his life. His anger built to the point that I didn't say anything. He cornered me against the wall in the dining room, grabbed both sides of my head, and banged my head against the wall thermostat several times. I don't remember anything he said."

Bonnie took a deep, quavering breath. "I was in shock, total disbelief. What had I done? He left and didn't come back until later that weekend. I put on a pretty outfit, got the house nice and clean, thinking this would help his mood. Not really. He basically ignored me. I guess I can just summarize a lot of stories. As the weeks passed, he would come home on weekends and the same things would occur.

"Once he accused me of saying bad things about his mother, which, of course, I don't think I did. Anyway, he got his rifle or shotgun and pointed it at Melanie, who was standing in her crib. He said that I had to get on my knees and beg for forgiveness about what I had said about his mother, or he would blow Melanie's brains out. I dropped to my knees, crying, begging for forgiveness.

"After that, I took the car which Bruce's dad had in his name, and I ran away to the preacher's house. That day or the next, I was told that there was a missing person report on me. So, I called the police and told them I was not missing, just hiding. They wanted to know where I was, and I said that I wasn't going to tell anyone. They informed me that they had a warrant for my arrest for car theft!

"So, I told them where I was, and yes, they came and arrested me. Bruce's dad had taken out the warrant. My dad came to the courthouse and paid my five-hundred-dollar bond. Later in court, the charges were dropped.

"Bruce got out of the Navy and went to work at a construction company. Over the months, I became more withdrawn. I can't remember all that time, but I thought maybe he was upset because he came home to a ready-made family.

"I constantly tried to think of things I could do better to improve his attitude. Maybe if he could be around the entire pregnancy, he could adjust, and it would make things better. During that pregnancy, he pushed me off the back steps, about 3-4 steps, and I landed on my stomach. I was so scared that it may have killed my baby, but all turned out well. April 11, 1969, Jeremy was born. I had the same feelings that I had experienced with Melanie.

"But things didn't change at home with Bruce. Bruce didn't make payments and some things were repossessed. He didn't pay the house payment, so my parents took back ownership of the house. I found a 3-room apartment; the babies, and I moved there. I think Bruce went to his parents'.

"While living in that apartment, I got the flu; I was so sick I could barely get out of bed. My mother came over to help, but, since my house was not as spotlessly clean as hers, she left, saying she just couldn't be in these filthy conditions. Bruce didn't help financially. The kids and I had little to eat, mostly grits and toast. My neighbor who lived on the other side of the duplex brought us groceries sometimes.

"When Melanie was one-year-old, she had to go to the hospital for malnutrition. I was so hurt and ashamed but didn't know what to do. When I went to visit Melanie, the huge head nurse put her hands on her hips and refused my visit. I wanted to knock her out of the way and go to my daughter. I felt like the world was all against me. So, I started praying.

"My childhood teachings came back. God would help, just ask, he cares for me. Ask and ye shall receive. After so many unanswered prayers, I gave up. I knew I had been brainwashed as a child and that God would not help and did not care. He was not the Santa Claus that I had learned about in church."

Bonnie paused. "I'm going to have a cigarette."

Carly said, "I'll get us some coffee, or would you rather have tea?"

"Tea would be nice, just a little sugar."

Carly's phone rang.

"Hey Carly, how's it going?" asked Thorne.

"You wouldn't believe it. It's going very well but her story, oh, you won't believe it. We're just taking a small break right now. What are you doing?"

Thorne said, "I went back to the street festival, talked a little with Josh. Tell Bonnie that he's doing pretty good, selling quite a bit, at least while I was there. I like him, he's one of the good guys, you might say."

Carly said, "I hate to cut this short, but Bonnie is coming back in.

"I'll tell her what you said." They hung up.

When Bonnie had her tea, they resumed. Carly said, "That was Thorne on the phone. He went to see Josh at the festival and said he was selling pretty well."

"Oh, I'm glad. He gets so anxious about it. It is so good when he sells a lot." She sipped her tea.

"You ready to continue?" Carly asked. Bonnie nodded. Carly turned on the recorder.

"Let me summarize a lot of it. Things stayed bad. The kids and I left several times, going back to my parents' house, which didn't last long. My mother would be understanding in the beginning but then, after a few days, she would say I had to make my marriage work. *Once married, always married; You make your bed rough; you have to lay in it.*

"So, I would go back to Bruce. Over the years, I had taken out several warrants for assault and battery on Bruce. Each time, I would drop the charges. We would try again, then repeat the same things. Finally, I couldn't take it. The kids and I moved to Rockway Avenue; later we moved to a three-room duplex on Carver Street. By the way, restraining orders are totally useless.

"One night before Christmas, I had taken the kids to see Santa at the mall. This was around 1970, I believe. We got home, I put the babies to bed. When I fell asleep, I was suddenly awakened by someone standing over me beside my bed. It was him. He started accusing me, asking me who I had been with. He was drunk and angry, out of his mind. He had his high school ring on his finger and when he hit me in the forehead with his fist, it cut a gash in my head.

"I was knocked off the bed. I was dazed momentarily and when I came to, I looked at him, knowing I had to trick him to hopefully change his mood. I said, "I'm so glad you came when I called. I fell off the bed and hurt my head." His personality suddenly changed to a caring husband. He got a washcloth for my forehead, helped me back on the bed. We talked and I told him how much I missed him and how we needed to be together. He believed those lies and left.

"He had parked his car down the road and had broken into my house through a window earlier that evening and hid under my bed. I called my dad and told him to call the police. My dad and the police came. Knowing the cops never did anything, when the policeman took out his notepad, I told him to put the damn thing back in his pocket and if he didn't do something, I would. My dad took me to the ER, where they stitched the cut on my forehead.

"The next morning, bandaged head and all, I went to the pawnshop. Back then, you didn't need a permit or anything. You could buy pistols right out. So, I bought one. I have no idea what kind, but I also bought a box of bullets. I went back to my duplex and waited. Bruce was due to come so we could get back together. When he knocked on the door, I was ready. I stood in the corner of the front room, facing the door, aimed the gun, and said something like, if you come through that door, it will be your last.

"Well, he broke into the door, and I aimed, pulled the trigger six times. Nothing. Just clicking sounds, except I think he messed up his pants. We went to court the following Monday. I don't know if he filed charges for me trying to kill him or if I filed charges for abuse. Anyway, Bruce was sent to jail for six months. When I think about it, knowing what I know now about guns, I'm sure with the bandage on my head, the pawnshop owner took the firing pin out of the gun. For a long time, I attributed it to angels keeping it from firing. Anyway, I guess you could say I had another head injury.

"God had not stopped Bruce from hurting me, or maybe He did help by not allowing him to kill me, or me him for that matter. Who knows, but I can say, I became totally disillusioned with my childhood teachings in church. I didn't want God in my life, if He couldn't help any more than that, I would have to help myself.

"I wanted to run away, find a new place to live, and start over. So, my parents agreed to keep my two children while I drove to find the right place. I think they were at their wit's end as well. I bought a Vauxhall car from my cousin, Josh, for $50. We didn't really know each other at that time. On my trip, I stopped in a few towns and checked out the towns' newspapers; no secretarial jobs, rent was too expensive, so I kept driving.

"Somewhere in the south of Georgia, my car broke down. There were no tow trucks or car repair shops that I knew about. I was in the middle of nowhere. So, I hitchhiked to the nearest town and rented a car for a daily fee and mileage charge. Thank goodness no deposit. I drove until I ended up in

Jacksonville, Florida. I only had about $40 and an Exxon credit card. I used my credit card and checked into a Holiday Inn.

"I don't remember the details of how a job and apartment worked out. I didn't get any sleep. I drove the rental car back to my parents and picked up my kids, put the few clothes we had in the car, and headed back to Florida. It was about a 10-hour trip one way. I surely couldn't do all that at this age. When I got back to Florida, the kids stayed with my boss and his wife, and I found a tow truck driver who would take me back to find my little car beside the road in Georgia." Bonnie paused.

"I really would like to leave out this part of the story; in fact, I have never told a single soul about it. But, since this information is for you to write a fiction story, no one will know it is about me. So here goes. We couldn't find my car, it was gone, maybe towed by the police, or stolen. So, on the way back to Jacksonville, the tow truck driver forced himself on me in the cab of his truck. No memories of any details or what I used for transportation after that. Back in Florida, it didn't take long for everything to snowball.

"No paycheck for a couple of weeks, no food, no money for rent or utilities; it was a mess. My boss and his wife, Wes, and Marie, I guess felt sorry for us and offered us to live with them until I could get on my feet. Marie kept my kids while I worked." Bonnie paused and asked, "This is going to be a fiction, right? I mean, you won't use my real name."

Carly reassured her.

Bonnie continued, "A month or so passed and one day I realized that I was pregnant. Desperate doesn't begin to describe my feelings at that point. Back then, the only place that abortion was legal was in New York. So, I lied to my boss and told him that my husband and I were going to get back together and asked if I could borrow the money to fly to North Carolina and drive back with him.

"He loaned me the money, so I flew to New York. I had never flown before; I was so scared. I took a cab from the airport to the clinic. The driver charged me much more than I think the actual amount of the fare. I numbly went into the clinic. The nurse counseled me a little, but there was no way I could ever change my mind. It had to be this way.

"Afterward, I didn't have enough money for plane fare back to Florida, but just enough to get back to Raleigh-Durham, so that's where I went. On the plane, I just stared blindly out the window, heartbreaking, crying the saddest tears of regret and shame and failure.

"Bruce had got out of jail a few days previously. I called him and told him I wanted us to get back together and that I was at the airport. He came to the airport, and we drove back to Florida. I'm not sure if I ever paid back the money Wes and Marie loaned me. I hope I did.

"Our little family was back together. Maybe Bruce had changed since he had spent time in jail. But, no matter, it had to be this way. I had nowhere to go and absolutely could not make it on my own with two kids.

"One wonderful memory I have about that time in Florida is that Roger Williams, 'Mr. Piano', was having a concert. When I made that album of my concert, I had sent him one. I don't know what I was hoping for. Later, I received a handwritten note from him personally, in his handwriting. I can't remember what it said exactly, but I was thrilled. I still have the letter in a box somewhere.

"Anyway, I went to his concert with a friend of mine. I gave a note to one of the ushers asking to see Mr. Williams and, in the note, I said that I had sent him my album. After the concert, the usher came to where I sat and said that Mr. Williams would see me. When I entered his room, my knees felt like Jell-O. We shook hands and I thanked him for his personal note and asked if I could use it on the back of my next recording. He said yes. I told him that I had dreamed of being a concert pianist and he said that I had what it took.

"I could have fainted on the spot. I was more than thrilled. I've never been a groupie or whatever you call the people who yell and carry on at concerts, nor do I swoon over other celebrities. This was different. I had loved Mr. Williams' piano playing since I was twelve. He is the one who played the *Warsaw Concerto* that I heard on the radio at that time.

"When I returned home that night, on cloud nine, I entered the pits. Bruce did not believe I had gone to a concert but rather was with some man. I became so depressed; I didn't want to live. But there was nothing I could change.

"I became pregnant again and on Mother's Day, May 12, 1972, I had Renee. Again, the feeling was the same as with my other two." Bonnie paused. "While I'm thinking about it. I remember when Melanie was older, she asked me how I could love her and Jeremy and Renee. I got four candles. I lit the first and said that the light is my heart full of love.

"I then took my candle and lit the first one and said, see, now Melanie, you have all my love and I still have love to give. I lit the next one and said, see, now Jeremy has all my love and I still have all my love to give. Then I lit the third candle and said, see, Renee has all my love and I still have all my love to give. If Sara had been around at that time, I would have lighted her candle to give her all my love as well.

"Anyway, back to the story; Renee was born on May 12, 1972, and I didn't see her as fast as I had my other two. I asked where she was, and the doctor solemnly told me that she had Down's Syndrome. He also informed me that she wouldn't live past her teens and that she wouldn't talk, nor would she ever recognize me as her mother.

"I immediately said that none of that mattered to me. I adamantly let him know that she is MY baby, and nobody would ever take her away from me. I cried and Bruce even shed a tear. When his dad saw her, he said that she looked like a bulldog. I hated that man for that.

"I loved Renee like all my kids and under no circumstances would I put her in a home. I was so sad for Renee. She was so precious. Why did she have to be different? Maybe she had to pay the price for my sin of having an abortion. I prayed to God again and again, but He never made her normal.

"Renee was slow in developing. She had to have special nipples on her bottles. She never cried, not when she was hungry and not when she got her shots at the doctor's office. She was just so precious. Melanie and Jeremy loved her as well. They would have protected her against anything, I believe. And, for that matter, still will. So, that was 1972.

"For the next couple of years, I was just a mother. I can't remember a whole lot about life except that I loved my kids. Soon afterward, I decided that the kids and I would go to church. It was a big church and the people were friendly. I felt a renewed hope in life, at least on Sundays. I had some good friends there too. I started praying that Bruce would change and we could be a happy family.

"During that time, there was a James Robinson crusade and Bruce attended one night. The message was so strong that Bruce went to the altar and accepted Jesus as his Savior. This was a little before Christmas. I was so thankful for this miracle and knew my life would be better and we could be a happy, normal family. I even have a photograph of Bruce sitting beneath our Christmas tree, reading the birth of Jesus story to Melanie and Jeremy.

"All was going well, but it didn't last.

"Sometime later, my friend's daughter babysat for us on occasion until my friend informed me that Bruce had sexually assaulted her daughter. The girl's father was away in the Navy, as many of my friend's husbands were at that time. It was too bad because the father could have put an end to all my troubles. But so be it. I guess it was better than no charges were filed, except, of course, for the girl. I wonder if she ever got over it. Back to the story. The abuse continued and so did the demanding sex. Bruce was at home very seldom. I thought he might be living part-time with another woman.

"I don't remember when exactly, but I wanted to die, there was no hope in my future. I tried calling a couple of friends, but they were happy and busy with life. I couldn't tell anyone of my desperation. I had no one to call. So, I got in my car and planned to drive off the Fuller-Warren bridge.

"On the way there, I remembered a psychologist who had preached or spoken at a little church I had attended a few times. I went to his office, walked in, and told the receptionist that I wanted to die, but first I needed to speak to Mr. Arnold. He immediately made time for me, asked me serious questions, and hypnotized me. He also taught me how to hypnotize myself with sentences of affirmation which I have done on occasion throughout the years.

"I must add here that it worked for all kinds of things, except for quitting smoking. Nothing has worked for that—not the patch, not the gum, not hypnosis, nothing, So, I smoke.

"Back to the story. My fourth baby was due, according to conception date, in mid-November, but when I went into labor, the doctor thought that it was too early, so he stopped the labor. Finally, late December, I had to have a Cesarean, the baby was too big. She weighed over 9 pounds and even had fingernails too—I knew those doctors had made a mistake about the due date.

"So, December 31, 1975, I had my fourth baby, a daughter named Sara. I was in the recovery room, so I didn't get to hold her immediately like with my other three. You are probably wondering why I didn't take birth control pills. There was no money to buy any.

"After the birth, I began having such excruciating pain that finally I wanted to throw the heavy, black, table-style phone through the hospital window and jump. The medical people wouldn't believe me, they tried giving me pain pills, enemas, thought I was just a crybaby or hypochondriac or something.

"Since I had had to have another surgery, my mother planned to come down to help take care of me and Sara. When she arrived at the hospital and took one look at me, she walked out into the hall and yelled, ordering the nurses to call a doctor, to *do something, my daughter was dying*! I guess that would be a good memory for my mother.

"Anyway, Dr. Brooks Brown came quickly, examined my abdomen, and gave me a shot of morphine—the best feeling in the world came over me. Just so happened, I had an intestinal blockage because when they closed the wound, somehow my intestines were crimped. Not sure of the medical explanation. So, I had another surgery.

"While I recuperated in the hospital, my mother took Sara home and took care of her. My mother became afraid of Bruce, and she got to see first-hand how he was never home. So, against the doctors' orders for bedrest, my dad drove down, and my parents took me and my four children back to NC to stay with them.

"When I was able, we returned to Florida, to hell on earth."

Bonnie got up, stretched. She looked at Carly. "Would it be possible for us to continue tomorrow? I'm pretty tired."

"Of course. I have planned the entire weekend just for you," Carly said and turned off the tape. "Let's sit outside for a while. You are welcome to stay here tonight if that would work for you."

Bonnie thought for a minute. "Are you sure? I know Josh is so tired after a show, he usually goes to bed early. I don't have anything else to do. So, yes, if you are OK with it."

"I'm positive, Bonnie. Let me call Thorne and tell him so he'll know he doesn't need to pick you up."

Bonnie said, "I'll call Josh and tell him."

Chapter Forty-Seven

The next morning, after breakfast, Bonnie and Carly sat quietly on the porch while Dinkle investigated the backyard. Carly broke the silence. "Whenever you want, we can continue where we left off yesterday."

Bonnie said, "You know, I used to dwell on all the traumas in my life. Since my life has changed, I've forgotten a lot of it. Maybe not forgotten some things, but there are large gaps in what happened, as well as the chronological order of some of it."

"That's understandable, I would think," Carly replied. "I think you are doing a good job with your story."

Bonnie asked, "Do you think you can write a book about it?"

Carly said, "I'm sure it's possible. I will need to decide on some of the details. I will, of course, make it a fiction with made-up names and places."

Bonnie finished her coffee. "I'm ready anytime you are, Carly," Carly called Dinkle and they went inside.

Carly prepared the recorder. Bonnie sat in her chair and began. "Let's see, where did I leave off?"

Carly said, "You were going back to North Carolina with your parents after Sara was born and you had had surgery for an intestinal blockage?"

Bonnie continued, "I think I need to summarize rather than go into so much detail. I want to get to the part that is better. Life's too short to spend so much time remembering all the yesterdays."

Carly said, "That's fine. Do it as you like, however you want."

Bonnie continued, "One of the frequent questions people ask is why I stayed, why I kept going back. I understand why they would wonder about that. I left high school after the tenth grade. I had no professional training. I could type, answer a phone, and so I got jobs as a receptionist or secretary, mostly. Back then, I believe minimum wage was somewhere around two dollars an hour. Daycare for four children cost more than I made. When you add rent and groceries, gas, insurance—well, you can see how impossible it was. Plus, after many years of being torn down, my self-esteem was very low."

Carly said, "I don't see how you made it. I can't imagine. I don't believe there are many people who could have withstood all that you went through."

"May be. So, to continue. Bruce and I got a divorce. Sometime in 1976, when living in Florida, I made my mind up to run away again. I had a yard sale. I called one of my cousins and he let me borrow $300. I bought three train tickets to Shelbyville, Tennessee. That is where my girlfriend from school lived. It just so happened she was going on vacation for a week and said we could stay in her house.

"So, on the train, Melanie, and Jeremy, and I took turns holding Renee and Sara. Trish's house was very nice. During that week, I bought an old Pontiac, I can't remember the price, but not much. I got a job as a receptionist at a realty company. I also tried to get some assistance, like food stamps or money just for a little while, a month or two, until I got on my feet. Well, that didn't happen. I found a trailer we could afford to rent. It wasn't that great but good enough.

"One day, this tall, good-looking man came into the realtor's office. I don't remember the details, but he and I got married in a short time. I was going to have another chance at being a good wife. After about a month, Jimmy, that was his name, drove up in the driveway but didn't come in. I met him under the carport. He informed me that he wanted to go back to his wife. He handed me $500 and drove away. I remember going back inside and Willie Nelson was singing *Blue Eyes Crying I the Rain*. In Tennessee you can get a no-fault divorce in 30 days. So that was that. Another failure.

"Not long after that, I was running out of money, no future in sight. I couldn't end up homeless. I have four children who needed so much more than I could ever give them. So, yes, I called Bruce. He came to Tennessee, and we remarried and moved to an old farmhouse outside of town. He had a job traveling, so he wasn't around very much, thankfully. Jeremy had a pet rooster. We also had a pet calf that we had to bottle feed. The calf thought he was a dog, laid on the porch and even accidentally came into the house once.

"I believe it was in January that Bruce decided we should move back to North Carolina, and he said he would go there and find a job and we could join him after that.

"During that winter, it snowed so deep that I couldn't go anywhere. A couple of ladies I worked with at Tullahoma Power brought us groceries. I was becoming desperate again.

"One day, I thought I was losing my mind. It was raining. I walked out the back door, walked down the long dirt road, and cried a prayer so loud, tears practically gushing out of my eyes, *Oh God, I can't stand it anymore. I can't stand it anymore. Life is hopeless.* After getting myself under control, and being soaking wet, I went back to the house. I call that one of my Scarlet O'Hara moments. When I got inside, I find out that Renee had peed on the cord to the small electric heater. So, no heat! A lot of good my prayer did.

"Well, we couldn't freeze to death. I lined chairs in a semi-circle around the fireplace in the living room and hung blankets on them to try to hold heat in from the fireplace. The walls in that old house had cracks that let in the cold and sucked out the heat. Not too long after that, I gave the calf to the landlord for exchange for rent. Jeremy's rooster had died.

"So, I packed up our things and headed over the mountain back to Durham." After a pause, Bonnie said, "I think I'll have a cup of tea; how about you, Carly?"

"Sounds good. You go smoke and I'll make the tea. I'll bring it outside and we can take a break."

They sat on the porch. Bonnie said, "You know, when I listen to myself telling all these things, I wonder what in this world I was doing; how did it all keep happening; was I crazy, head injured? I don't know. I just know that I'm here today and I made it through all of that."

Carly didn't say anything. After a while, they went back inside, she said, "OK, you were on your way back to North Carolina."

"Right," said Bonnie. "Traveling over the mountains was scary but we made it. We lived in a house on Duke Street. The driveway sloped down toward the carport. I was always scared that my brakes might fail, and I would run into the house. Times in that house were no better, even worse, if that was possible. I don't remember all of it. The thing that ended it all to me was when Bruce forced himself on me; I was a zombie, dead inside. In my mind, that was the final straw. In 1978, we were divorced, again.

"The kids and I moved to a nice apartment in the Barcelona complex. I still lived in constant fear. I had a job and taught piano part-time.

"When it was time to get car insurance, I went to the agency. I looked much older than I do even now. I had no self-esteem, no self-confidence. The agent who wrote my policy happened to live in the same apartment complex and invited me to go out for pizza. I thought, super, my kids can have pizza.

"After we ate, I took the leftovers home to them. The agent's name was Allen. To make a long story shorter, he invited me over, fixed me tea, and I told him a little about my situation. He was about 14 years older than me. He had a daughter and son, close to my age. I felt more like a friend to them than a stepmother. I guess he liked lost causes because I spent quite a bit of time with him. I also had my first drink of alcohol. I didn't like it except for the way it helped me not feel so sad.

"One night, Bruce put sugar in Allen's gas tank. Allen went out and confronted Bruce. They fought, the police came, and I don't remember what happened. All I know is that I had found someone who took up for me and wasn't scared of Bruce."

Chapter Forty-Eight

Bonnie continued. "One day, Jeremy and Melanie came to me and said that they wanted to go live with their daddy. I was shocked but understood because life with me was full of responsibility that a child should not have. I also knew that when they spent time with their dad at his parents' house, they had fun and got to do things that were so different than they experienced with me. After I got over the shock, I thought that maybe it would be good for them to see that when they were with their dad for more than a day or two, things would not be so much fun. So, I called Bruce and told him.

"He came to get all four of them. I was certain I would get a call the next week telling me that they wanted to come back. But the next thing I got was a court notice of a hearing for Bruce to be granted full custody of my kids. I knew beyond a shadow of a doubt that that was impossible. I mean, Bruce had over 16 arrest records for assault, and battery, and had been in jail. No judge would award a sick, dangerous man custody of my four precious children.

"At that time, I was working at an engineering firm. I got time off to go to court. I had a corporate lawyer, not one who practice domestic law. No problem, the judge would see and make the final decision." Bonnie paused a long time.

"We can take a break, if you want," said Carly.

"No," Bonnie said. "I need to get through this part." She continued, "We went to court, the usual setting. Bruce had a few witnesses from his work. I had no one. Anyway, the verdict came from the judge. 'Custody is awarded to the plaintiff'. You could have not done more harm to me if you had shot me with a gun. The judge found me to be unfit for custody. I didn't cry. I went to the ABC store, bought a fifth of Smirnoff vodka and went to my apartment. All I remember is that I sat on the floor at the end of the couch, and drank, and drank, passed out, came to, and drank more.

"After three days, my phone rang. It was my boss, wondering what was going on. I told him I would be back at work the next day. So, in a daze, I returned to work. I thought I had felt hopeless before, now I knew despair, total darkness, no future. I remember taking the children's belonging to them at

Bruce's parents' house and Jeremy came out to the car to get the bags. He didn't speak, just slammed the car door. For a long time, I would hear that slamming door in my mind.

"I didn't care anymore about anything really. I worked, I ate, I slept, and visited Allen's more often. He smoked marijuana and when he offered it to me, I took it. When I was younger, I had watched the TV show, *Dragnet*, and remember the deadly effect of drugs. But I didn't care anymore. What did I have to lose, my life?

"So, I learned to party. Allen would talk about reality in a different way than I had ever heard. He took me shopping and I bought some stylish clothes and bathing suits. No care about the cost, whatever I wanted. I began to look prettier, healthier, and happy, even if it wasn't through and through. I lost at least ten years in my appearance.

"At some point, Bruce was moving to South Carolina and, of course, taking the kids with him. So, we would meet halfway for me to have my weekend with them. I was so overjoyed to see them but at the same time, so heartbroken to see them go.

"One Friday, when we met, I said something to Sara about the fact that I was glad she had called; I don't remember what it was about. Bruce immediately ordered the kids back into his car. They started crying. He drove off. My heart didn't crack, it completely broke. Hopelessness returned. Something inside of me changed. I guess it was self-preservation or survival. But I became indifferent, or cold, I guess you could say. My heart lost its ability to feel anything that resembled caring or warmth or even love. I would not put my kids through that torture again, so I didn't see them for a long while.

"Meantime, Allen, and I married. We moved from the apartment into the house my dad owned, the same one I started living in back in 1967. Life was one party and a blast after another. No care in the world. I still cried myself to sleep most nights, however." Bonnie got up without saying anything and went outside.

Carly turned off the recorder. *That was what the journals were all about*, she thought.

Carly wanted to hug her. Her own heart could feel the pain. Then she remembered her own birth mom.

When Bonnie returned and sat in her chair, she said, "This is harder than I thought. After some time thinking back over things, I knew my boss at that time was drinking buddies with Judge Reed. I also think my boss wanted to have an affair with me. I accused him years later of influencing the judge, but of course, he denied it. I'm not sure I believe him. He died not too long after that."

Bonnie continued, "Around 1983, I believe it was, Melanie wanted to come back and live with me. She was of age to say where she wanted to live, and I had a husband with a good income. Oh, that reminds me, my mother thought that Allen was in the mafia or sold drugs because who else could make that much money. So, one day, I took his paycheck stub and showed her. I think she was even jealous of that.

"We went to court. The judge gave me custody of Melanie and Jeremy but not Renee and Sara. I don't know how to describe my feelings about that. How can you have a broken and happy heart simultaneously? Just split in two.

"The time with Allen was grand for Melanie and Jeremy. They got stylish clothes, they loved it. Allen bought Melanie a 1967 red Mustang, her dream. All was fine, or at least half fine. I worried about Sara and Renee constantly. Melanie would go visit them and tell me about the awful living conditions. Sheets stained with pee, hair not cut or combed, lots of bad circumstances. What could I do? You know there were many times, I thought of killing Bruce. I even conjured up ways to do it but knew I couldn't go to prison and leave my kids.

"Melanie found a guy she loved and moved in with him. I reassured her that if it didn't work out, she could always come back home, which she did. I told her at that time, that after age 18, if it didn't work out, that she was on her own. I regret saying that. I never wanted her to feel not wanted or not loved. But I also felt that she needed to learn to stand on her own two feet.

"My life with Allen lost its luster. I no longer enjoyed partying. I felt lonely most of the time. One day, I told him to leave. He did. So, then it was just Jeremy and me."

Carly interrupted, "In your journals, I remember reading about Allen shooting himself."

"Yes, he did. I can't remember exactly when that happened in the scheme of things, except that it was while he lived in the Barcelona complex. All I know is that he changed at some point. His ego had been hurt, I guess. He raised his hand to me one time, that's when I sent him away, which I could do because we lived in my parents' rental house. I wasn't scared of him, just knew that no violence would ever be tolerated by me again. Ever! So, we were divorced."

Bonnie paused a minute. "As I tell you this, I may have gotten things out of order. Some things are jumbled up as far as the timing goes. I can remember where I lived at the time of most things, but maybe not the exact order they happened."

"That's quite OK, Bonnie." Carly understood.

Bonnie continued, "Melanie married Billy. They had two wonderful kids. I was still living in my parents' rental house. The partying stopped after I told Allen to leave. I was working, Jeremy was in school.

"One day, I came home from work and Jeremy and his friend were sitting on the couch, smoking pot, watching TV, oblivious to reality. Something came over me. I looked at Jeremy and told him to go upstairs and pack his clothes and get out. It was raining but I didn't care. He did that. I sat on the floor at the foot of the stairs and cried. I wondered if I had made another huge mistake. He had to learn some responsibility and that life was not all parties and fun. I didn't hear from him for some time.

"The big change for the better, I might add, came into my life quite my accident. My mother called me one day saying she had somebody at her house that needed to talk to me. She thought that since I had been through so much, I could be supportive.

"So, when I got to their house, I found it was my first cousin, Josh. We ended up going for a ride in his truck. He sipped alcohol from a bottle under his seat. I hoped I had not made another mistake by getting in the truck with him. We talked. His wife had thrown him out because he wouldn't quit drinking. She was, according to him, a Christian and wanted him to change his ways. I told him that I knew all about judgmental, sanctimonious Christians. Since Jeremy had left, I had an extra bedroom, so I told Josh that he was welcome to stay with me.

"The next day, he came and brought only a few possessions; his clothes, his pistol, and rifle. I'll just summarize a little of this story. Josh and I lived our separate lives. He worked and I worked. He went out on weekends, and so did I. As time went on, we came to be close friends. We would sit around on Friday and Saturday nights, have a few drinks, talking about life and things we believed. I told him some things about my life also.

"One day, he came down the stairs on his way to work. He was dressed in a light-colored suit. I saw him as a man, you might say, not my cousin. I was attracted to him in a female way. As time went on, we became close. He took me fishing and camping. I had so much fun. I love to fish even now.

"One day, Melanie called me and said that she had found a Steinway grand piano that she wanted me to see. I can't remember, but I think it cost around $3000. I bought it and I was so happy. That had been one of my childhood dreams. I called and told my mother, thinking she would be happy for me too. Well, later that week, she called, and her words were, 'You can take your precious piano and get out of my house'. That weekend, Josh and I found the house in Bunnlevel, the one you now live in, Carly. and we moved in.

"We camped, went fishing, and Josh taught me to shoot. I loved that. When I fired his Ruger, I felt the power, the control, the fear left, my personal world changed. I was an excellent shot too. Josh called me Annie Oakley.

"Josh taught me to hunt deer. When deer hunting season came in, Josh put up my tree stand in the game lands near Butner. It was raining that day and I had on a pair of rain boots that were a bit larger than my size. So, when climbing the tree, I slipped.

"I immediately thought about the tree-steps ripping my whole body open and pushed off the tree. Josh had warned me to never carry my rifle when climbing, but to pull it up on a rope. I didn't do that, so, when I fell, I landed on my back on top of my rifle. I couldn't move. I managed to turn over to my stomach but couldn't crawl either. I knew I was paralyzed. No one was around. I lay there for quite some time.

"Finally, deer hunting dogs found me, the hunter came and called 911. The EMTs took me to the hospital; I had broken my back. I wore a brace for a long time. Josh was so upset that he hadn't stayed closer to where I was.

"When I got better, we went hunting on a friend's land. When we arrived at his house before dawn, there were 2-3 older men sitting around the table having coffee. One of them said, "You mean you're gonna let her in the woods with a gun?" Everybody laughed.

"At my hunting site, I sat on the ground—no tree stands for me, thank you. That day, I shot a buck and a doe. When Josh and I were headed back to the friend's house with the deer on the back of a pickup, I hollered to the three old men, "Next time, I'm gonna put a bullet in my gun!" That was my last hunting trip. I had accomplished it and knew I would never starve to death. Time for another break." Bonnie went outside.

She began talking as she came back inside. "I've taken up your entire weekend."

Carly replied, "No worry. This is working out great. We still have tomorrow. I'll split the royalties with you when I become a number one bestselling author."

Bonnie relaxed and continued. "OK. Well, during this time, Melanie visited Jeremy, where he lived in South Carolina. When she returned, she told me that Jeremy was not living in a good way. There was no food in the house except for a bag of frozen French fries, and he slept on a mattress on the floor. I felt I had to do something.

"Josh and I went to where Jeremy was living. He didn't want to come back with us, so we left after giving him some money to buy food. But a few blocks away, I told Josh to turn around. I was determined that Jeremy was coming back with us. He did. When we arrived home, I told Jeremy that he was going to get prepared physically to join the Army. He did. I think it didn't take long for him to realize that Uncle Sam was a different parent than he had known. I personally believe that his time spent in the Army was good for him.

"Sometime later, Sara called me. She told that she had been abused by her stepbrother and no one cared or believed her. She was crying and I told her I would do all I could to get her back. So, again, a shorter story. I went to the lawyer who had the reputation of being mean and getting results in the courtroom. He said that it would cost $5,000. I told him I would have it that afternoon. I went to my parents, and said right out, I need $5000. My dad got this let's-think-about-it expression. I blurted, this is not a request, this is a demand! I was determined. They gave me a check made out to the lawyer.

"The lawyer filed the necessary papers, whatever it took. I rode with him to South Carolina. He was old, half senile, didn't know how to operate all the buttons in his Lincoln, and very used to getting his way with the judges in Durham.

"Well, it was a different story in South Carolina. He had no pull with anybody, and he was not even allowed to represent anyone in their court. So, I was appointed a lawyer from South Carolina. I don't remember his name. All that I know is that he was one sharp cookie. He put Bruce to shame and the judge had no choice but to grant me custody. Now my heart was completely healed. I had all four of my children out from under that monster."

Bonnie paused. "I'm feeling a little hungry. How about you?"

Carly said, "Yes, it's about supper time. Let's see what we can eat. We have a variety of things to make a salad."

Bonnie said, "I'll help."

After eating, Bonnie went outside to smoke, and Carly took Dinkle out.

Carly said, "We can finish all this tomorrow, if you'd like."

Bonnie said, "I'm close to the end and would really like to finish it tonight, if that's OK."

Carly said, "Fine. We can do that. And you are welcome to stay the night."

Bonnie said, "I know Josh can't come get me and I don't want to bother Thorne."

Carly said, "Thorne surely doesn't mind. Let's see how it goes and then decide."

Bonnie agreed.

Carly, Bonnie and Dinkle went back inside, and Carly turned on the recorder.

Chapter Forty-Nine

Bonnie began, "It took some adjusting for me to being a mother again. Sara and Renee had been gone so long. They didn't know me, and I had changed so much. I didn't want Sara to make any bad decisions. She had learned how to tell lies while living with her dad and I didn't allow that.

"One day, rather than being understanding and kind and patient, I told her that if she lied again, I would send her to her dad's, thinking this would certainly make her tell me the truth. I can't remember the details, but after that, she lied about something, and I took her to the bus station with a ticket to her dad's house in South Carolina. Later, I called to make sure she had arrived, but she had not. She never did.

"Panic, fear, regret, all the emotions you can imagine, came over me. For the next five weeks, I searched every waking minute. The police said that she was probably at a friend's house, and they didn't do anything. The last place she was recognized by a bus driver was in Fayetteville, same city where my sister and her family lived. They said that they had not heard from her.

"Finally, after intense investigation on my part, I found out where she was and went to get her, brought her back to my sister's house. My sister suggested that I leave Josh, so Sara could be happy. No way. That's not how I do things. Anyway, Sara came home. Soon after she went to live with Melanie, during which time, she met her future husband, a wonderful man, I might add. They have three children and are still very much in love.

"Jeremy got out of the Army. He is now married to an exceptional woman, Jean. They have four children. Jean home-schools them. They live in Colorado and are doing good. I just wish I could see them more often.

"Renee lives with me, of course. She is 49. She has taught me so much about patience and understanding. A pure human being in every way. She forgives instantly, doesn't hold grudges, and is very tidy and organized. She senses things too. All my children are so precious to me, but I guess I would have to say that Renee holds her own special place in my heart."

Bonnie took a cigarette break. When she returned, she continued, "Josh and I had decided to open an art gallery downtown. A lot of preparation had to be done and city ordinances passed. It was beautiful. We opened it late in 1993. I enjoyed running it. It was filled with Josh's art as well as mine. We met the expenses every month. We stayed motivated and inspired. I still did medical transcription and ran the gallery."

Carly said, "I believe some authors record their writing to be transcribed."

"I did it for doctors and various medical facilities. I was self-employed for most of the time. I believe listening to recorded tapes of various voices every day contributed to my hearing loss. I wear hearing aids.

"Now, where was I? OK, the gallery. In the spring of 1994, the world crumbled. I left that morning to open the gallery. At the intersection not far from our driveway, a lady in a Jeep Cherokee ran a stop sign and T-boned my Nissan. That was, of course, the wreck in which Thorne's wife died."

Bonnie paused. "I wasn't wearing a seatbelt, thank goodness, and was thrown across the front seat. I don't remember much. The highway patrol came, and I gave them our phone number and they called Josh. I was taken to the ER. They removed glass from my face and other parts of my body. The next thing I remember was a little later when I developed a severe headache and went to see my private doctor, who ordered an MRI of my head.

"Aneurysms were seen and my doctor referred me to UNC, Dr. Estrada Bernard. He was the perfect doctor for me. He was patient, understanding, and my surgery was scheduled, I believe, for the first of June. My parents, kids, Josh, and his brother were there. The surgery lasted 13 hours. I don't remember much except that I was bald-headed with a huge ugly scar on the side of my head."

Carly had tears in her eyes. "All this is unbelievable. How a person can suffer through so much in life. You are a strong woman."

Bonnie said, "Like I told you about my opinions changing over the years, well, I finally took a little of the initial blame on myself. My hardheaded stubbornness and rebellion are what got me started on this path. Although, I wish my mother had known better how to deal with me, that's just not the way it was.

"All those years of being strong, determined and ways to survive ended after my brain surgery. I couldn't think, couldn't count change, my short-term memory was completely gone. If I dropped anything, I had to pick it up immediately or I would forget that I had dropped it. I couldn't cook anything complicated, only a simple one-dish meal, mostly microwave food.

"The neuropsychologist tried me on several medications for ADHD and other things to help. I didn't like any of them. The last one I tried was *Concerta*, which worked great. I was smart when I took it. But when I didn't, I couldn't do the things I did when on it. For a few years, I would take it when I had to think clearly. Then I quit it.

"I have done everything possible to help my mind. I play games, I read. My memory still isn't like it used to be, but I think it is as good as it is going to get. I don't like taking any medicine, really. I use essential oils, old-timey remedies as much as possible. I believe my body is made to heal itself of most things. Of course, the medical profession is nice to have for things like intestinal blockage and brain surgery."

Carly asked, "Did you have any therapy or rehabilitation?"

"No, I had no insurance, so I guess they didn't bother recommending it. I did have vision problems. My peripheral vision was greatly diminished. I saw an ophthalmologist who told me that I may go blind because my retina had been damaged. I tried to plan for life as a blind person. But thankfully, I didn't lose my eyesight and I'm thankful for it every day.

"Soon after I got back home to Josh's, my parents decided I needed to come live with them to recuperate. So, my sister and her husband came and loaded up my things, took me to my parents' house. They all told me that Josh didn't really love me, he was just using me. As I would believe anything at that time, I believed what they said and cried all the way to their house. After my brain surgery, the main things I can recall are things that affect me emotionally.

"Soon, I moved to a rental house on Shenandoah Avenue. I somehow acquired four cats. I was asked to leave the rental house because of the cats and the owner didn't want that smell in her house. Amazingly, I could still do transcription work.

"I moved back in with my parents. My belongings, furniture like my favorite chair, and rugs I had crocheted were put out for the trash pickup. More of my mother's control. I don't remember much of the order of events for many years. All I did was type and make it one day at a time.

"My parents found a cute little bungalow type house about three miles from them on Acadia Street, and they helped me with the initial $1000 earnest money up front. I bought it for $52,000.

"Josh visited on weekends. Like I said, I don't remember much. During my time there, I tried playing the piano at the church I attended as a child. That was short-lived. I started reading and studying the Bible. I would go over to my parents almost daily and discuss the things I was learning.

"One day when I was at their house, my mother told me to *Get a life*. I only visited occasionally after that. When I think about it, I'm sure they had had enough of me. After attending several churches in my life, I think churches are corporations for making money, and people attend to be social or to gain business contacts. Also, I think most preachers have psychological issues.

"I listened to tapes by Hal Lindsey which I enjoyed. I began to understand that God was not Santa Clause. It's hard to explain.

"On day, I was lying on my couch, and I whispered the name '*Jesus*' several times. I think the medical profession would say I had an auditory/visual hallucination. But I know differently. I felt cocooned in a soft cloth in the clouds. I said aloud, *"My Abba, my Abba."* I felt totally different inside.

"The next day, when reading the Bible, I came upon the verse about calling out those exact words. Bible believing people would say that that was my confirmation of what I experienced, and I agree. Since that time, there has been absolutely no doubt that I am a child of God's. Also, from Hal Lindsey's teachings, I began to understand about God's Will. There is His Passive Will and Perfect Will. You will never stop being His child, no matter what.

"All this led to me seeing my life differently. I wanted God's Perfect Will for my life, so I knew some things had to change. I explained this to Josh and told him that we could not be intimate anymore unless we were married. We went to South Carolina and were married. I would have to find the marriage certificate to tell you the date. I would guess maybe ten plus years ago. We have in total been together about 35 years. He would still come on the weekends because he couldn't stand to live in the city where I did. He loves the woods, nature, hunting, fishing, and all that.

"We spent a couple of years looking for a place to buy. Then one day, I found the house we live in now. You can't believe the miracle that happened in purchasing it. The owner was asking $72k. After some back and forth, changing our mind and everything, we ended up offering $42k. The owner accepted. So, we moved and after some adjusting to the move, we have been totally happy. The first Thanksgiving, we had the whole family, my parents, brother and sister, and my children for a wonderful meal and time together." Bonnie paused.

Carly said, "I would very much like to meet your family, besides your sister, obviously. How about your brother? Do you think he would like to know about me?"

Bonnie said, "I don't know why not. I'll let him know about you and see what he says. He is gay. He and his partner live in Florida. I would love for my kids to meet you. They are super and I'm thankful every day that I have them in my life. I'm so proud of all of them. I always told them that they had every excuse to use for not doing their best, like some people would do. They are my life."

Carly said, "Maybe after my wedding in September, we can arrange a get together."

Bonnie said, "Maybe at your wedding. That would be nice. A huge family reunion at the beach."

Carly said, "Would you like to go outside for a while?"

Bonnie said, "Yes. Let me just sum up a little bit of all this long story. I know I made some horrible mistakes and misjudgments along the way. I have been misjudged by others. I also know that I turned totally away from God and everything I was taught and believed as a child.

"But, like the Bible teaches, that nothing can separate you from the love of God once you accept Jesus as your personal Savior. The part about the Perfect and Permission Will of God, I understand a lot better now. I don't push my belief on anyone. If I'm asked, I say faith is a personal issue. There is a song that says it all. It's *Through It All* sung by Andrae Crouch.

"I guess you would say that He has been with me through it all, watching me mess everything up that I tried to fix.

"My favorite Bible verse is: *Trust in the Lord with all your heart and lean not on your own understanding; In all your ways acknowledge Him, and He shall direct your path. Proverbs 3:5-6.*"

Epilogue

Carly and Thorne were married on the beach in September. Bonnie's entire family, except for Kathleen, was there. A lot of Carly's and Thorne's friends also attended. It was a most joyous occasion. Nellie was the best Maid of Honor ever.

Neither Carly nor Thorne would say where they planned to spend their honeymoon, but everyone knew Thorne had it all planned perfectly.

THE END